This edition,
signed by the author,
is limited to
500 copies,
of which this is copy
number

205

BRIGHT
LIGHTS

BRIGHT LIGHTS

The Duchess of York

DELACORTE PRESS

Published by
Delacorte Press
Bantam Doubleday Dell Publishing Group, Inc.
1540 Broadway
New York, New York 10036

Cataloging-in-Publication Data is available from the U.S. Library of
Congress.

ISBN 0-385-32178-3

American English has been used throughout this book.

The text of this book is set in 14-point Granjon.
Manufactured in the United States of America
November 1996
10 9 8 7 6 5 4 3 2 1
BVG

To my best friends,
Beatrice and Eugenie

Dear Reader,

I am delighted that you are about to read my newest book projects—two companion novels about the delightful escapades of an adventurous princess and her look-alike friend.

The Royal Switch and *Bright Lights* are novels about Princess Amanda, a mischievous redheaded girl who lives in an elegant world—a world into which I have special insight—and her desire to break free from its constraints. Her friend, an American eleven-year-old named Emily, who is *not* a princess, understands how it feels to face disappointments and then to bounce back and seek good times again.

It is my hope that this energetic pair's engaging adventures, set against the colorful backdrop of two dynamic cities—London and New York—will win your heart.

As the mother of two young princesses, I know the importance of reading and sharing books. I remember how much I loved to be drawn into books that swept me away to enchanting places and took me on exciting adventures. It is thrilling to be able to write stories that can be read not only by my own girls, but also by wonderful young girls all over the world, girls like you.

I hope you will have as much fun reading *The Royal Switch* and its companion, *Bright Lights,* as I had creating the stories for you.

Sincerely,

Sarah, The Duchess of York

BRIGHT LIGHTS

Chapter One

Emily Jane Chornak raced up the stone steps of her Brooklyn Heights brownstone and burst through the front door, through the hall, and into the living room.

"Mom! Mommy! Maaaa!" she called.

"Calm down, Emily," her mother answered. She came to greet her daughter from her office, which had been converted from a guest room.

"Where's Dad? Is he home?" Emily was almost panting.

"Yes, he's here, of course." Emily's mother gestured behind her. "We're making the last-minute arrangements for Sunday night."

1

"Okay, okay." Emily flopped down into an overstuffed armchair and leaned her head back. "I just wanted to make sure you were both here. You know, to greet Amanda when she comes."

"Well, of *course* we'd be here, what do you think?" her mother said with a smile. "It isn't every day a princess spends the weekend in our humble abode! Besides, we work here, so where else would we be? How was school?"

"Mom, I figured you'd be here. But I never know—you could be anywhere! Flying around the world, auditioning new talent, checking out *old* talent—whatever it is you and Dad do! School was fine, but it was hard to keep my secret. I promised Amanda I wouldn't tell anyone she's a princess. I had to zip my lips! Can I have a piece of candy?" She shook her curly red hair out of her eyes and it caught the light, gleaming like splashing sunbeams. "I've been a good girl."

"Have some fruit instead," her mother said.

"But first you should read the fax that came for you just this minute. It's on Dad's desk."

Emily sat up straight. "*What*? A fax?"

"Yes, a fax."

Emily was on her feet. "Oh, no! Oh, *no*! She's not coming! She's not coming! Oh, Mom, do you think Amanda can't come? Why didn't you tell me the minute I came in?" she wailed.

"Emily Jane, read it first before you get hysterical. I haven't even had a chance to look at it."

"Oh, Mom . . ."

"Emily, go into the office and read the fax before you talk about doom and gloom."

"I'm afraid to know."

"Well, fine, then. You'll never know."

"Oh, Maaaa . . ."

Emily trudged into the office her parents shared. It was a busy-looking room with tapes and CDs strewn everywhere. Papers were everywhere, too, as well as a fax machine, two computers, telephones, and walls lined with pictures of—it seemed to Emily, anyway—almost everyone who had ever made a musical recording or appeared in a concert. Emily never looked at the pictures. She was unimpressed with the fact that her parents were agents for well-known musical artists. Their work left them with little time for *her*. The stars always wanted more and more attention. Emily had once heard her father say, "They're worse than children!"

"Daddy, where's my fax?" she asked.

Her father was sitting with his sneakered feet propped up on her mother's desk, reading the newspaper.

"Hi, Em, how was school?" he asked, but before she could answer, he called out, "Helen! What page did you say the ad ran on?"

"School was fine," Emily said. "Where's my—"

"Oh, never mind! I found it!" her father

continued. "It's not bad, not as well placed as it was in the *Post,* but it's okay. Helen, isn't Liza's name supposed to be in the ad, too? I can't find it!"

"Daddy! I'm talking to you!" Emily shrieked. "My fax from Amanda!"

"Sorry, Em. Here." Without taking his eyes from the newspaper, her father handed her a sheet of fax paper. "No, no, it's here, I see it. Mmmm . . . 'Luminaries from every part of the music world, from Pavarotti to Madonna'—Hey, I love that, Helen, that's good! What a night this's gonna be! We'll raise a bundle for a worthy cause."

"I can't believe this," Emily wailed.

"Helen!" Emily's father yelled.

"Don't yell at me, Daniel, I'm right here." Emily's mother stood in the doorway. "So what did Amanda write, Emily dear?"

"Look at this!" Emily's father waved the newspaper. "Another robbery of jewelry and art—this time the Beckwith place. That's the

5

third robbery this month! And aren't the Beckwiths coming to the concert Sunday night?"

"Who cares about a jewelry robbery?" Emily said. "*I've* been robbed. Don't you care about me?"

"Now, Emily, let's try to deal with the situation, whatever it is. Tell me what's in the fax," her mother said calmly.

Her father finally put his paper down. "Em, I'm sorry, honey. You know how I am when I'm wound up about something. Now, what's the matter?"

Emily took a deep breath, then sighed. "Well . . . Amanda *is* coming . . ."

"Great."

"But . . . her parents won't let her stay here with us."

Emily's mother drew herself up to her full height. "What do you *mean* her parents won't let her stay here? What's wrong with us, I'd like to know! What's wrong with our house?"

She swept her arm around the messy room. "I mean, Amanda is a princess by birth, but she's still a little girl, ten going on eleven years old. Because she happens to be a princess doesn't mean she has to be isolated from real people!"

"It *does* mean that, Mom." Emily sighed again. "Amanda can't go places the way a regular kid can. *She's* upset about it, too. I guess that helps me feel a little better. She says that's why she didn't telephone herself; she was too upset. Anyway, what she says is—"

"What?"

"She says she'd like for *me* to stay with *her* at their hotel. They're staying at the Continental Regency." Emily let her hands fall to her sides and looked at each of her parents. "Her driver, Jack, will pick me up at four-thirty today if it's okay with you."

"Oh, really!" her mother sniffed. "Let me see that fax."

"Mom, Amanda doesn't think we're not good enough or anything, it's just that posh

7

kids can never do anything they want! *Please* let me go. I know it's short notice, but it's a once-in-a-lifetime adventure. You and Dad always drop everything and run when famous people invite *you* somewhere."

Emily watched her mother react to her words and recognized the signs of a mother giving in.

"You are great!" Emily cried. "I'll never—well, maybe never—give you a hard time again. Ohmygosh! It's late! Jack will be here in an hour! I'd better get packed!"

"No, wait, Emily," her mother said. "Listen, first call Amanda at the Continental Regency and we'll tell her we agree and that we'll drive you in. They don't need to send someone for you. Go on, call. Or I will." She nudged Emily toward the telephone.

Emily frowned.

"It's the proper thing to do," her mother said.

Emily made the call. Her mother tapped

her foot while the two girls chatted happily away on the phone, excited to be talking again after their London adventure.

"Ask her!" Emily's mother said encouragingly.

"Now, Helen, you just want to meet Amanda's parents," her husband teased.

She answered in a whisper, "So do you!"

Emily put her hand over the mouthpiece. "She says Jack is already on his way."

Emily's mother pursed her lips. "All right," she sighed, "but look, tell Amanda I want to talk to her mother for a minute. I'd like to invite the Prince and Princess to the concert Sunday night at Carnegie Hall. *Everyone's* going to be there! After all, it's a benefit for New York's homeless."

"Okay." Emily repeated the message into the phone, then stood tapping her foot. After a few minutes she listened again to the phone, said, "I see. Well, certainly. Okay," and hung up.

9

"Emily—"

"She said her mother said thank you so much but they're so terribly busy while they're here and, besides, Amanda's nanny got hurt or something at the airport and they're all in a big tizzy about that."

"Hmph!"

"So okay?" Emily said. "Jack'll be here any minute and I have to pack a bunch of party dresses."

"A *bunch*?"

"Don't worry about it—if I don't have the right stuff, I can always borrow something from Amanda!"

Chapter Two

"*H*iiii-iiii!"
The two girls screamed and threw their arms around each other's necks as if they hadn't seen each other for years. Actually it had been only a little more than a month.

"Amanda!" came a voice from another room.

Amanda hunched her shoulders and put a finger to her lips. "We must be quiet," she said softly. "Nanny still needs a great deal of rest. But, oh, come in, Emily! Come into my room so we can talk! Jack's brought your things in already."

They bounced together on the canopied four-poster.

"I'm so sorry I couldn't come to your house and stay with you," Amanda said. "I really wanted to!"

"I know. We were all disappointed. I had planned a weekend that I thought you'd like—being a typical American preteenager! But at least we're going to spend the time together! Jack was great! He explained to my parents that your parents didn't want to inconvenience them."

"Lovely!"

"They were bummed that your parents can't make the benefit concert they've organized. It's a huge event." Emily made a face. "As my dad says, 'Every star in the *galaxy* will be there!'"

Amanda's eyes widened. "*Every* star?"

Emily laughed. "Yes, Princess, *every* star. Even your favorite group, the—"

"—Mashed Potatoes!" Amanda finished. "Oh, I do wish we could go . . ."

"Me too." Emily sighed. "And I bet *they* wish you'd be there, too!"

"*They?*" Amanda cried, her eyes bright. "You mean the Mashed Potatoes know I'm in New York? They want to see *me?*"

Emily held up her hand. "Amanda, I honestly don't know if those guys know you're here. *I* don't get to talk to them; only my parents do. But I remember the fabulous time we had when you sang with them when I was in London!"

Amanda blushed as red as her hair and flopped back against her pillows. "Emily, I think of that incredible night so often," she admitted, staring up at the canopy. "It was brilliant! There I was . . . on the stage with the best rock group in all of Britain . . ."

"And *singing* with them, too!" Emily finished. "I bet if you weren't a princess, they'd have hired you!"

"Oh, Emily!"

"I mean it, Amanda! You have a fantastic voice! And when you sang 'Rocket to the Moon'—"

"I *love* that song!"

"I could tell. You really added something. Seriously! You did those funky harmonies— I mean, I saw their faces when you started singing. The group never expected anything like that, I'm sure. Not even from a princess!"

Amanda smiled. "*Especially* not from a princess." She sighed.

"Amanda?" Emily looked around and moved closer, lowering her voice.

"What?"

"Did you ever tell your parents? I mean, do they know we went to that little club with Jack and my parents? Do they know you actually *sang*?"

Amanda put a finger to her lips and shook her head. "They know that we went out with your parents, of course, and that it was part of your parents' business that week in London. But I never mentioned—"

"—that you nearly turned professional!"

"—that I sang with a famous rock group, no."

Both girls laughed.

"They probably wouldn't have believed me anyway," Amanda finished.

"Probably not."

"And they *definitely* would not have approved."

"*Definitely* not!"

Emily changed the subject quickly. "What happened to Nanny? It's not anything serious, is it?"

"Serious enough. She broke her leg getting off the airplane. Caught her heel in the carpet, she said. They set the leg in hospital and now she's only just got here in an ambulance. The airline's taken care of everything, and the doctor's given her something to help her sleep."

"Wow."

"Yes, well, she'll be laid up here in the hotel the whole weekend. She doesn't want to fly back on her own."

Emily looked around to make sure they were quite alone. "Amanda—does this mean *we'll* be on our own? You know . . . without Nanny chaperoning us?"

"I can never be without a chaperone, Emily." Amanda sighed. "But it's all right. We'll have fun anyway. Mummy and Daddy really brought me on this trip so that they could spend time with me, and you and I will have each other when whatever they're doing gets boring for us."

"What *are* they doing?"

"Well . . ."

There was a soft knock at Amanda's door. "Yes?"

Megan, the young lady-in-waiting, stood in the doorway.

"Excuse me, Princess. I've brought your frock for tonight."

"Thank you, Megan," Amanda said, nodding at her.

"Will you be needing my help dressing?"

Amanda shook her head. "Thank you, no, Megan. That will be all."

The young woman curtsied and closed the door.

"Help *dressing*?" Emily repeated, and giggled. "I forgot what it's like to be a princess! Let's see what you're going to wear!"

"Let's see what *you're* going to wear!"

The girls compared dresses. As they chattered away, they decided they were *not* going to look like twins this time. When they had met in London, they had been similarly dressed, and with their bright red, curly hair, freckles, and blue eyes, they really had been hard to tell apart. Even Nanny, Jack, and Emily's parents had been surprised!

But tonight they would look different. Emily would be wearing a green printed dress with a white collar and shiny black shoes. Her mother had fastened her hair with a pretty silver clip before she'd left home. Amanda was in pink again, this time a pink jumper over a lace-trimmed white blouse. Her hair was loose, flowing past her shoulders.

"Guess they like you in pink, huh?" Emily said.

Amanda sighed. "It's ladylike," she said. "I'm expected to be ladylike."

"Well, you are. Sort of."

"Thank you for the *sort of*," Amanda said, laughing.

"Where are we going, anyway?" Emily asked. "You started to tell me."

"Yes, right. You mentioned that your parents were running a really posh benefit concert this Sunday to raise money."

"It's for a good cause, but both of them have been walking around with their ears glued to phones for weeks! They're producing this event almost by themselves, but they've spoken only five words to me since it started: 'How was school?' and ' 'Night, honey!' "

"My parents are here to raise funds, too. They have a full schedule of social engagements planned for this weekend to try and encourage Americans to make donations."

"What for?" Emily asked.

"For the National Portrait Gallery's roof. It was practically blown off in a windstorm, and the gallery needs a new one."

"The National Portrait Gallery's *roof*?"

"Yes, private donations are required, since the ratepayers mustn't pay for the repairs. It's full of priceless pictures—some are my ancestors—and if too much rain gets into the building, everything will be ruined. No one will be able to replace them."

Emily nodded.

"So my parents are here to attend parties," Amanda went on, "and we'll have a brilliant time together."

Chapter Three

The dinner at which Amanda's parents were to appear that evening was at a restaurant in an elegant hotel on Manhattan's Upper East Side. Emily remembered her parents talking about this well-known, extremely expensive, "in" place.

At the arrival of the Prince and Princess of Powers Court, Emily noticed, people turned with interest. The Prince and Princess—and Amanda and Emily behind them—were greeted, smiled at, and bowed to all the way to their table. They all smiled and nodded in return—except for Emily, who wanted to dive under the table.

Once they were seated, Emily saw, everyone seemed to have pasted on a smile, but there was silence all around.

Emily coughed and sipped water. Her hand was shaking, and some drops fell on her dress. Quickly she reached for her napkin to wipe her lap, and she felt her face growing as red as her hair.

Amanda, who of course looked completely calm, gave Emily a reassuring look.

The Princess, Amanda's mother, cleared her throat ever so softly. "Tell us, Emily, what form are you in at school?"

"Well—"

"I believe the word here is *grade*," the Prince corrected his wife politely.

"*Grade.* Yes. I'm in the fifth." Emily tried to answer calmly. "Fifth grade. Or class. Whatever. I mean, whatever you like!"

"Do you study languages, my dear?" the Prince asked.

"Well . . . not foreign ones until junior

high," Emily answered. The Prince and Princess glanced at each other. Amanda, Emily knew, studied French and German and was tutored at home.

"My favorite subject is English," Emily said. "I mean American English—I mean, language arts. . . ." Her voice trailed off. "I also like social studies and math."

"How lovely," said the Princess. "Now for the menu."

"I would like the lamb, my dear," said the Prince. "What do you think you'd like?"

Amanda turned to Emily and whispered, "We never eat together at home. My parents are not used to talking to children."

Emily smiled weakly.

Suddenly a beautifully dressed couple appeared at the Prince's elbow.

"The Powers Courts! How lovely to see you in New York again! And what a perfect time of year for your visit!" The gentleman seemed to gush all over Amanda's parents. The Prince rose courteously to greet the couple.

"We've just come from cocktails with the Beckwiths," the lady said to Amanda's mother. "Althea's mother's sapphires were stolen from her home, and one of her Cézannes was taken off the wall, and no alarms went off!"

"No!" Amanda's mother exclaimed.

Emily sighed, relieved that the attention of Amanda's royal parents had been drawn away from her. "I think your parents hate me," she whispered to Emily.

"Don't be a goose," Amanda answered. "You're an American. My parents still don't understand why you didn't want to remain a British colony!"

Both girls laughed.

"How's your cousin George?" Emily asked as she examined her place setting to be sure she picked up the right silverware.

"Oh, my cousin George! You would mention him!" Amanda snorted. "Ever since his birthday party he's been just so nice to me! I'm still wondering what you said to him when he thought you were me."

"I thought he was nice." Emily shrugged.

"I know. Now he thinks *I* think he's nice. I say, what do you think, should we ring up some of those American tourists I met on your tour?"

Emily put down her bread. "They were awful! Especially that Debbie. From Detroit."

"Debbie was fun!"

"Amanda?" The Princess was peering at them. "You must keep your voice down, my sweet."

"I'm sorry, Mummy."

"We'll have to speak with some of these people after dinner. Will you young ladies be able to amuse yourselves quietly while we circulate?"

"Yes, Mummy."

"Lovely."

Emily looked from one grand person to the other, wishing she could find something witty to say. *Her* parents had loved everything Amanda had said when they'd met. And they had been very curious about Amanda's parents. Maybe the Prince and Princess would want to know about *her* parents, too. Maybe grown-ups were only interested in other grown-ups.

"My parents were disappointed that you can't make the benefit Sunday night at Carnegie Hall," Emily said at last.

The Princess smiled. "Yes, we were, too. What . . . exactly is it that your parents *do* again, Emily, dear?"

"They're artists' representatives!" Amanda piped up. "It's so exciting, Mummy, they know all the *best* groups! The Evil Weevils, the Mashed Potatoes, the—"

"How nice," the Princess interjected.

"Not just rock groups, ma'am," Emily

added. "I mean, they handle opera stars . . . and classical musicians, too."

"That must be very interesting," the Princess said, looking at the Prince out of the corner of her eye.

Emily decided to change the subject. "I'm looking forward to showing Amanda New York. There are so many wonderful places, but I guess you know about New York already. I hope you don't think New York is a bad place just because we've had a lot of big robberies lately. I mean, there are *little* robberies, too, but I meant the ones the newspapers have been writing about. . . ."

The Princess looked at Amanda and then turned to Emily. "You and Emily will get to see the city. Now eat up your salads while we chat with the people at that round table. Keep your voices low. We'll be back in a moment." She got up and moved toward the round table in the middle of the room. The Prince rose and followed her.

"Emily, don't get the wrong impression from Mummy," said Amanda. "My parents just don't understand theater people. I mean, they know who someone like Barbra Streisand is, but they don't keep company with entertainers."

"Do they *like* Barbra Streisand?" Emily asked in a small voice. "Because my parents know her manager. . . ."

"Emily." Amanda touched her friend's hand. "Don't be hurt because my parents aren't very friendly. They're the same way with me!"

"Amanda, darling!" The Princess suddenly reappeared at the table, startling both girls.

"Yes, Mummy?"

"There's someone special here for you to greet. Constance Potter. You remember Mrs. Potter?"

Amanda thought, but before she could answer, her mother said, "She visited us once or twice at Powers Court. Or perhaps it was at Howard Hall. She would adore to see you."

"Me?" Amanda glanced at Emily, who shrugged.

"Now be your lovely self, darling," the Princess said. "Mrs. Potter is very much interested in the National Portrait Gallery's roof, and she could be most helpful to our project. Come along now. You too, Emily dear. We mustn't leave you alone at the table."

The Princess steered Amanda and Emily across the room.

"Constance!"

A tall woman with sleek blond hair and diamond earrings in the shape of swords turned to greet them.

"Why, it can't be Princess Amanda! How you've grown!"

Emily winced.

Amanda held out her hand. "How nice to see you again, Mrs. Potter. I'd like you to meet—"

"Oh, I can see you've brought one of your dear cousins along on this trip!"

"Actually—"

"My, my, my, the family resemblance is so *strong*!" Mrs. Potter gushed. "Look at that fabulous red hair on both of you! And the shapes of your faces, as well as—"

"Constance, actually this is Amanda's American friend, Emily." The Princess quickly corrected the misunderstanding.

"Friend?"

"Yes, from New York," Amanda added.

"New *York*?" Mrs. Potter sniffed. Emily could see that Mrs. Potter was disappointed she wasn't a royal cousin. Emily was sure Mrs. Potter was an American, but she spoke almost like Amanda's parents. She acted as if she was trying to be English.

"I live in Brooklyn Heights," Emily put in.

"Emily's parents are, ah, in the arts," the Princess said, gracefully sweeping a strand of hair from her forehead with her fingernail.

"Really," Mrs. Potter said.

"Yes, they—" Emily began, but Mrs. Potter ignored her.

"How nice for you to have a local friend to share your time with us, Princess Amanda," she said. She smiled at Amanda's mother. "You know, my daughter, Tiffany, is the same age as these lovely young ladies. I would have brought her this evening, but I didn't know children were invited."

"No, you were quite right, Constance," the Princess replied. "This is not a children's affair. However, Emily is here to share Amanda's time with us. But tell me, my dear, when were you last at the Portrait Gallery? I don't think you've been to London since Easter, is that right?"

Mrs. Potter frowned. "I believe I saw the portrait of Lady Havemeyer being hung in the West Wing."

"The West Wing!" the Princess of Powers

Court exclaimed. "Well, my dear Constance, the West Wing has been flooded!"

"No!"

"Yes! I'm afraid we had a near-total collapse of the roof over that section!"

"Would it be rude to go to the rest room?" Emily whispered to Amanda.

Amanda moved to her mother's side. "Mummy? May we please be excused?" she asked sweetly, being sure to smile again at Mrs. Potter.

"Of course, darling. Constance, dear, you just can't imagine—"

Amanda and Emily moved out of hearing range.

"Are all these people here for your parents' fund-raising thing?" Emily asked.

"I believe so," Amanda said, steering Emily toward the back of the restaurant.

Emily grabbed Amanda's sleeve and covered her mouth to stifle a giggle.

"What?"

"Look," Emily said, trying to keep her voice low. "Check out that woman right next to the wall. Two tables down. Under the chandelier. See?"

"Oooooh!"

"What is that on her head, a peacock feather hat or a dead chicken?"

Amanda squinted. "It's a turquoise cap with rhinestones and a feather on top. Isn't it silly!"

"I want to see the rest of her getup," Emily said. "Let's check her out as we go by."

"Don't laugh, though," Amanda cautioned. "Remember who we are."

"Who *you* are, you mean," Emily answered. "Nobody here cares who *I* am."

"Oh, Emily, that's not what I meant—"

Emily grinned. "I was only kidding. But don't worry, I won't do anything dumb."

"Now, whom do you suppose the feather hat is with?" Amanda asked, peering at the woman out of the corner of her eye.

"Two men . . . ," Emily said as they walked slowly in the direction of the rest room. "I feel like Sherlock Holmes! If one of them is her husband, the other one is too old to be her son. Very strange."

"Maybe he's her brother," Amanda guessed. "Or a close family friend."

"Very good, Watson!" Emily said. Then she pretended she had dropped something and had to pick it up. "The younger guy is cool-looking, isn't he? Look, his hair's slicked back. He reminds me of that actor, you know, the one in—"

"Shhh! We're getting awfully close," Amanda warned.

Nonchalantly they walked past the feather hat's table, trying hard not to stare.

"Wait a sec, Amanda!" Emily said in a harsh whisper once they had passed the table.

"Shhh! What?"

"Look under the table," Emily managed to

mouth, moving her lips but not making a sound.

Amanda craned her neck as Emily grabbed her arm to pull her away.

"Don't be so obvious," Emily commanded.

"How can I see under the table if I don't look?"

"Just keep walking with me," Emily ordered. "She's got turquoise *shoes,* and she's kicked them off under the table!"

"You saw that?"

"Yes! I saw her wiggling her toes!"

"My mother would be horrified!" Amanda said, holding a hand over her mouth. "Nanny would faint dead away!"

"You can see for yourself on the way back from the rest room. Come on, we'd better go or your parents will start to wonder what's keeping us."

"They won't worry," Amanda said confidently.

"I'm sure they'd be concerned," Emily said.

Amanda nodded toward the front of the restaurant, and Emily followed her glance. Jack gave them a friendly salute.

"You really are watched all the time, aren't you?" Emily said.

"Told you," Amanda retorted.

Riding back to the hotel in the limousine, Emily listened as the Prince and Princess commented upon the evening and discussed whether or not they'd been successful at raising funds.

Amanda leaned her elbows on the plush armrests and yawned. "I'm so-o tired," she sighed. "I'm really still six hours ahead of you on London time."

"I forgot about that. And I thought I was tired!" Emily said. "It's like you haven't slept at all in almost two days!"

"Nanny made me go to bed early all last week to prepare for this week, but I guess I kept going on all the excitement."

"Your parents don't look tired at all," Emily whispered.

"They're used to jetting around. They always fulfill their responsibilities. They have their job to do and they take it seriously. Of course, tomorrow they'll probably lie in until noon."

"What will *we* do then?"

"A supervised *tour*! Oh, Mummy!" Amanda wailed. They were back in the hotel suite.

"Amanda!"

"I'm sorry, Mummy," Amanda said softly, and dropped her eyes.

Emily flashed back to the moment in London when exactly the same thing had happened to her. Because her parents had been so busy, she had been pushed off on a bus tour with a bunch of kids. This time, she and Amanda planned to have fun. After all, a tour of New York City had to be better than a grown-up fund-raising party.

The Princess said, as if reading Emily's mind, "I would think you'd enjoy seeing New York instead of sitting about in your hotel room. Especially with your friend along."

"You're right, of course, Mummy. I would," Amanda said.

"We won't need Jack to be on call with the car," the Princess said as the Prince took her wrap from her shoulders, "because we'll be resting until very late tomorrow afternoon. So he will take you."

"Jack?"

"Yes, Amanda."

"Not a tour bus?"

"A *tour bus*? Heavens, what could possibly have put *that* idea into your head? Now, Megan will help you get ready for bed. Good night, my sweet. Good night, Emily, dear." The Princess swept off toward her rooms, followed by the Prince.

When the lights were out and Megan had left the room, Emily whispered, "Amanda!" across the gap between their beds.

"What is it?" Amanda murmured sleepily.

"Are these sheets silk?"

"Mmmm, I think so. Why, are you allergic?"

"No, I just wondered. I can't wait until tomorrow! Won't we have fun?"

"Mmm-hmm. Emily, do you know New York City well?"

"About as well as you know London, but I don't know about the personalities. I mean, not as well as you know about Queen Victoria. I remember the details you told me about Victoria, Albert, and London during her reign. All that history you explained to the kids on the London tour? When they thought you were me? Remember, Amanda? Are you awake? Amanda . . . ?"

Chapter Four

I n the backseat of the limousine, Emily mar-
veled that, with the windows closed, the
ordinary New York City noises—sirens wail-
ing, horns honking, taxi drivers yelling, dogs
barking, street musicians playing, and car
alarms shrieking—simply vanished. She knew
the noises were still out there, but she couldn't
hear a thing.

This is weird, she thought. But then, sitting
in a limo next to a princess who looks like
me—or is it that I look like her?—is pretty
strange to begin with.

Emily blinked. Jack, the chauffeur and se-
curity man, was saying something; he was ask-

ing Amanda where she wanted to go. His accent wasn't at all like Amanda's or her parents'. They spoke beautifully. Jack sounded different, and Emily liked listening to him, too.

"I'd like to see everything, Jack!" Amanda was declaring. "The Statue of Liberty, the Empire State Building, the United Nations, Broadway, Museum Mile, Central Park, SoHo, Greenwich Village, Madison Avenue—all that and more!"

"You forgot about Rockefeller Center, where they put up the huge tree at Christmas-time and you can ice-skate under the golden statue of Prometheus," Emily reminded her.

"Oh, yes! Lovely!" Amanda said.

"That's where the NBC television studios are," Emily added. "We have so many channels to watch here—not just the BBC."

"Will we see any stars from the telly, do you think?" Amanda asked, wide-eyed.

Emily almost laughed, but she controlled

herself and said, "You know, Amanda, to most people *you* are as exciting as a TV star. You're a princess, after all."

"Let's not discuss that," Amanda replied crisply.

"The new dinosaur exhibit at the American Museum of Natural History is a right topper," Jack said helpfully from the driver's seat.

"How do you know about that?" Emily asked.

"Jack accompanies my father on his travels and knows heaps of cities," Amanda explained. "Jack has many special talents—that's what Daddy says."

"Wherever you'd like to go, young ladies," Jack said, "your wish is my command."

"Cool," Emily said.

Amanda clasped her hands together and held them under her chin as they stood at the prow of the ferry approaching the Statue of Liberty.

"I've seen only pictures . . . ," she whispered.

"We can climb up to the crown if you want," Emily suggested. "It will be pretty crowded in the summertime, but there aren't so many people here today. The seven points of that crown represent the seven seas and continents," she added proudly.

"Really?" Amanda asked.

"You know all about your Queen Victoria, and I know my Statue of Liberty!" Emily said, grinning. "Actually, the lyrics of some song my parents played over and over and over last year included that bit. I can't believe I finally got to use that information!"

Amanda gasped at the panoramic view from the statue's crown. Emily, although she had been there twice before on school trips, also exclaimed at the scene. Amanda was delighted that she'd be able to say she'd seen New Jersey, another of the fifty states.

They reboarded the ferry, which was now

heading to Ellis Island and the immigration museum and family history center. Emily watched Amanda's glittering eyes taking in the Manhattan skyline.

"There's no place like the Big Apple, huh?" Emily said.

"Oh, yes, but it's more than just the fantastic view," Amanda said.

"What do you mean?"

"I was just thinking," Amanda said, and laughed. "I'm having such a lovely time with you that I wish this day could go on forever."

"Finding a friend like you does seem like a dream." Suddenly Emily glimpsed something out of the corner of her eye. She frowned.

"What's wrong?" Amanda asked.

"Well . . . Don't turn around, but— Amanda, I said don't turn around!"

"Oh, Emily, it's a reflex, don't you know? If you say to someone 'Don't think about elephants,' what do they think about immediately?"

Emily laughed. "Okay, but I didn't want him to know we saw him."

"Who?"

"This boy. *Please,* Amanda, don't look at him, okay?"

"All right."

"It's a real grungy-looking boy, and he's watching us. He's kind of leaning against the doorway, you know, where you can go sit inside if you want."

"How do you know he's watching us?" Amanda asked.

"I can tell, believe me. He hasn't taken his eyes off us this whole time."

Amanda held up her hand, and Jack was instantly at her side.

"Emily believes there is someone staring at us, Jack," Amanda whispered.

"Where?"

Emily turned to show Jack. "He's— Hey!"

"What?"

"He's gone. He isn't there anymore."

"Maybe you were mistaken, Emily," Amanda suggested.

"Please describe this person, Miss Emily," Jack said.

"He was . . ." Emily thought a moment. She recalled the boy's face. Actually, his eyes hadn't looked at all nasty or frightening—only eager, curious, and sad. The way he'd looked at her and Amanda . . . there was something about him.

She shook her head and said, "You're right, I probably imagined it."

"Are you quite certain, Miss Emily?" Jack looked concerned.

"I don't think it was anything to worry about," Emily said. "I really don't."

"If you see him again, Miss Emily . . . ," Jack said, and Emily nodded.

Amanda, Emily, and Jack stood together in the Registry Room, where large black-and-white photographs showed exhausted immigrants waiting in line after line as they

48

arrived in America at the beginning of the twentieth century.

"See the top of that stairway?" Emily asked, pointing.

"Yes?"

"That's called the 'staircase of separation,'" Emily explained. "People had to walk down those steps to get on ferries. Some went to Manhattan and settled there, some headed to the West, and some were made to go to detention rooms right here on the island."

"Detention rooms?"

Emily nodded. "Can you imagine? Some people weren't allowed into the country after their long trip here. Those rejected were put on boats and sent right back to wherever they had come from."

"That sounds *horrible,*" Amanda said. "Why were they sent back?"

"I read that some of the people had medical problems," Emily explained. "Maybe they had a bad cold when they arrived, or head lice, or a cough. If there was the slightest thing wrong with you, you got sent back. There were doctors here to make sure no one got in who was sick."

"Oh, my." Amanda sighed.

"My teacher had us research Ellis Island before we came here on our class trip," Emily said.

She was interrupted by Jack, who cleared his throat and politely directed her and Amanda to move along.

The girls walked on, and Amanda quietly told Emily, "Jack doesn't like me to get too close to other people. I'm supposed to keep safely away and not stand out in the open." She giggled suddenly. "You can imagine how upset my London adventure made Jack and everyone." Then she added, "I think Jack's afraid I'll be kidnapped. I used to be frightened, too, but I've learned to be calm but cautious—usually!"

"Wow," said Emily. "Your life is so weird—I mean different."

"I'm used to it. Although I'm sure there isn't anyone outside my family who knows who I am when I'm on a public outing. Of course, if it's a special occasion and all my relatives are in attendance, that's different. Otherwise, nobody pays much attention to me."

Emily got a funny feeling in her stomach and peered around, wondering whether the raggedy-looking boy she'd seen on the boat might have followed them. She saw no sign of him. Other tourists were studying the American Immigrant Wall of Honor, where the names of immigrants were listed alphabetically.

Nobody is paying any attention to us, Emily told herself. We're just two redheaded girls with a grown-up chaperoning us. And without Nanny here to guard Amanda, Jack takes his responsibilities very seriously.

But when they were back on the ferry, Emily spotted the boy again. And he was watching them! She drew in her breath and was about to alert Jack when the boy flashed her a smile.

It wasn't at all a scary smile. It was warm and friendly. Then the boy waved.

This boy can't possibly know who Amanda is, Emily thought. He's not a lookout for a kidnapping gang. He's not a criminal. He's just a kid like us. She knew her mother wouldn't have approved, but she smiled back. The boy grinned, nodded, and turned away.

Once they had gotten off the ferry at the southern tip of Manhattan, Jack drove them to the 110-story World Trade Center. They took an elevator that shot up to the observation deck in seconds. Amanda said the view was brilliant. Then Jack drove them to the eastern side of southern Manhattan for a stop at the shops and museum of South Street Seaport.

He hurried them through the Seaport, looking nervous.

"Too many people," he said when they were in the car again.

"Do you think it's too risky to go to Times Square, then?" Emily asked. "Honestly, it's a sight to see."

"The theater district?" Jack said. "Oh, I think that will be all right. It's not our West End, of course, miss, but Times Square is quite a fascinating place—especially when the neon lights go on at night. I'll drive by the area. There will be no getting out of the car, though, I'm afraid."

He drove them along West Forty-seventh Street, as well as Forty-eighth, Forty-ninth, and Fiftieth, and all along Broadway and Seventh Avenue. In the heavy traffic, the big car moved slowly, and Emily stared out the window at the city she'd known all her life. She could almost hear her mother's voice: "It hasn't always been this bad. We must do something." There was a man sleeping on a pile of shopping bags in the side doorway of a theater. Probably everything he owned was in those bags, Emily thought. That's why her parents were doing the benefit. When Emily had been younger, she'd never seen this many people just sleeping right there on the street. That man, he'll be chased away pretty soon, Emily thought. Tourists come to the theaters. They don't want to see men like that. . . .

"I want to see that show!" Amanda cried. "Oh, that one played in the West End!" She was looking up, reading all the theater marquees.

"You'd probably see a lot of the stars if you could only come to the benefit my parents have organized tomorrow," Emily said. "The musical stars, anyway."

Amanda sighed. Both girls knew that Amanda's parents would not allow it. Emily decided not to bring up the subject again.

At the 102-story Empire State Building, the three of them went up in another elevator and exclaimed at the view from the observation deck. "There's the United Nations!" Emily said.

"The people on the pavements look like ants," Amanda said, "and the cars look like toys!"

"Time for tea, I think, Princess," Jack said.

"Let's have tea at the American Museum of Natural History!" Emily suggested. "They've got a place to eat called the Garden Café. Or we could have a snack in the Diner Saurus!"

"Yes, let's!" Amanda agreed.

"We're off, then," Jack said, "to Central Park West and Seventy-ninth Street." Emily laughed. Jack was obviously pleased with his own knowledge of New York City.

Off they went uptown. But along the way Jack headed southward on Fifth Avenue for a few blocks in order to pass right in front of

Rockefeller Center and St. Patrick's Cathedral before heading uptown again.

"Do you think New York is as nice as London?" Emily asked, sure it was a hard question to answer.

"I think it's all quite lovely," Amanda said. "I love to be out and about."

"Spoken like a true princess," Jack said over his shoulder from the driver's seat. "A tribute to your parents' training in diplomacy," he added, smiling.

Chapter Five

They had their snack in the Diner Saurus at the American Museum of Natural History and then walked up to the Theodore Roosevelt Rotunda and saw the skeleton of a huge dinosaur.

"What is it?" Amanda asked.

"It's a barosaurus," Emily read aloud from the descriptive card. "It's a female. Look, she's rearing up like that because she's defending her baby."

"One of her fossilized neck bones weighs almost two hundred pounds!" Amanda said, reading over Emily's shoulder.

"Quite a pain in the neck," Jack said, and both the girls groaned.

"Come on, this isn't even the new dinosaur exhibit," Emily told them. "Let's go up on the fourth floor!"

The skeleton of *Tyrannosaurus rex* was enormous.

"Does that remind you of anyone you know?" Amanda asked.

"My parents' lawyer." Emily laughed.

"Look at those ribs! They're so long they could be the bars of a cage we could fit in!"

They moved on, staring at the enormous ancestors of birds and beasts and stopping at the interactive computers set up throughout the exhibit room.

"The leg bones of apatosaurus remind me of my great-aunt Lois," Emily said.

"That skeleton of the head of triceratops looks just like a rhino," Amanda pointed out. The girls loved watching how the jaws went up and down.

"I hope the scientists are wrong about being

able to bring dinos back to life with DNA," Amanda said. "I wouldn't want to find them strolling about Powers Court!"

"No one can bring dinos back to life really," Emily said indignantly. "Can they, Jack?"

Jack rolled his eyes and rocked on his heels.

"No, they cannot!" Emily emphatically declared. "Come on, Princess Amanda, your family has crown jewels and all those treasures, but you're going to want to see the gem room here. Not just because of the gems, but also because it's a great place to wander around."

"This *is* the best room of all!" Amanda cried as she saw the many-leveled space.

The girls pointed and exclaimed over a six-sided amethyst from Sri Lanka; a quartz stone from Brazil as big as a grown-up's hand; a coral necklace from Taiwan; rock crystal, chalcocite, adamite, azurite, and all the other startlingly colored and strangely named minerals on exhibit. Emily's favorite was the Star of India. At 563 carats, she read, it was the world's largest blue star sapphire. The brilliant white star sparkled in the center of the stone.

"I love this one," Emily said. "I wish I could have it."

Amanda laughed. "Even if you could own it, what would you do with it?" Then she looked thoughtful and said quietly, "It's not always easy, owning precious things." She yawned and stretched. "You know, I'm getting tired. I think it's time to go back to the hotel."

"Certainly," Jack said.

The girls walked from the gem room toward the exit. As they passed the special exhibit in gallery 77, Emily touched Amanda's sleeve.

"What is it?" Amanda asked.

"He's here again."

"Who?"

"The boy we saw on the ferry. Wait, wait, please don't call Jack yet."

"I must tell him, Emily—"

"I know, I know, but listen—I think that boy just likes us or something. It's not because it's you."

"I can never be sure, Emily. I've been made aware of so many situations that can lead to danger."

Emily bit her lower lip. "He's not out to hurt us. I just know it."

"I'd better have a look at him," Amanda said.

"Yes. Turn around. He's the one wearing clothes about a mile too big."

Amanda turned and spotted the boy. At her glance, his face lit up. He cocked his head shyly and moved his hand, almost waving.

Amanda nodded politely and gave him a quick smile.

"You're right, I think. He seems to be alone. He does seem harmless, but we never take chances. I still must tell Jack." Amanda held up her hand.

"I know. I'd never want anything to happen

to you." Emily sighed. "How old do you think he is? About thirteen? Fourteen? I think he's cute. Amanda?"

Amanda was quietly telling Jack about the boy and indicating with her eyes where he was standing. But when they turned around, all they saw behind them were museum visitors peering into glass cases.

At the hotel the Prince and Princess were dressing for their evening party. The girls were to accompany them.

"It's a gallery showing," the Princess explained. "Contemporary portraits, which I don't much admire, but the Prince will speak about our efforts on behalf of the National Portrait Gallery in London. We must attend. I thought you'd want to be included, Amanda."

"Yes, Mummy. How's Nanny?" Amanda asked.

"Coming along. I do wish she were here for

you girls. Nevertheless, there's nothing for it but to muddle through. Emily, my dear, your parents rang us while you were out. They personally invited us to their little musical event tomorrow evening. Lovely of them."

"May we go, Mummy? May we?" Amanda took a breath. "May we go to the benefit, please? It would be so much fun to be all together. . . ."

"Darling, I've explained that our time is completely taken up on this trip. Emily's parents certainly understand. Now you must get ready. I don't think we need to arrive late."

"What will *we* do, Mummy? Emily and I?"

"Be charming to all the guests. Look them in the eye, shake their hands politely, tell them how delighted you are to meet them all. You know what is expected, darling."

"But, Mummy, maybe Emily and I—"

"Darling, you'll be with us. You'll look at the exhibition. You'll have a delightful time. How was your tour of the city?"

65

"It was super! I've learned so much. Mummy, did you know that no one really knows what color dinosaurs were when they were alive?"

"Oh . . . ," her mother replied vaguely, "that must have been fun." She snapped a compact closed and added, "Run along and get ready. Megan will help you; she's laid out your things and something for Emily if she needs appropriate attire."

As they entered the gallery on Madison Avenue, Emily heard the sounds of laughter, music, low voices, crystal glasses tinkling against one another. Emily was familiar with the sounds. This sort of party was part of her parents' life as well. Emily shrugged. She knew some kids thought this was exciting, but she'd rather have been watching TV.

She stayed close to Amanda as they greeted people. The adults bent low to shake her hand. It looked as if they were bowing. Perhaps they are, Emily thought. After all, Amanda is a real princess!

Amanda always introduced Emily as her special American friend.

Emily listened to the conversations swirling around them:

"Malcolm and I summered in Italy this year. Have you been to the superb . . ."

"Are you going to the benefit for the homeless tomorrow night? It's not only a worthy cause, of course, but I hear there's going to be a fabulous lineup. The Chornaks are producing, you know. . . ."

Emily felt proud when she heard her parents' names mentioned. As jealous as she was of the time they spent on their work, it still gave her a good feeling to know that her mother and father were doing a great job. She looked over and saw Amanda busy with someone in a blue dress.

"Have you seen what's-his-name's new show? Honestly, my dear, it's hilarious!

There's one scene where . . ." Emily continued to try to follow the many conversations.

"Isn't that Claire over there, Beanie? The
one in the velvet. Now there's a woman who
should never wear green!"

"Try one of these, sweetie, I think it's
duck."

"Yes, he died, right in the middle of Rich-
ard's speech. Don't you find that terribly in-
considerate?"

"Have you heard? There was *another* robbery last night. The Sneads' mansion! Dickie
told me they lost a beautiful . . ."

Emily sighed. Chatter, chatter, chatter, but
what were they talking about? There were too
many people around, and no one really seemed
to be listening to anyone else. Emily wondered
what some of the guests would say if they
knew she was the Chornaks' daughter. The
Prince and Princess might see that around
here, Emily was almost like royalty herself.

The hors d'oeuvres were tasty, especially the little tarts, but she was getting hungry for a real dinner.

As Amanda touched Emily's sleeve, she whispered, "Look what's coming our way," and winked.

"Good evening." A familiar-looking tall woman in a beaded black dress walked up to Amanda. "Remember me? We met again last night. I'm Constance Potter," she said brightly, and gave a small curtsy. Emily bit her lip as the woman tried to bend her knees in her tight dress.

"I'd like to introduce you and your friend—"

"Emily," Amanda said politely.

"Emily. Yes. Well, I'd like you to meet my daughter, Tiffany. She's just your age!"

A girl with straight blond hair, wearing a fancy dress, stepped out from behind Mrs. Potter.

Amanda held out her hand graciously and smiled as she said, "It's a pleasure to meet you, Tiffany."

"A pleasure to meet *you,* Princess," Tiffany replied, and imitated her mother's curtsy. "Oh, and you, too . . ."

"Emily," Amanda prompted.

Emily gritted her teeth and managed to mutter, "Charmed."

"I'll just leave you young people to get acquainted," Mrs. Potter said, and fluttered off before anyone could say anything.

"Have you walked around the gallery yet?" Amanda asked Tiffany.

"A little," Tiffany answered with a yawn. "Mother says they're not terribly authentic. The artists made the people look so much better than they actually look." To Emily, Tiffany sounded just like Mrs. Potter—like an American trying to be English.

"Let's go have a look," Amanda suggested to Emily. "Maybe we can figure out who the real people are. I'll bet some of them are here! If you'd care to join us, Tiffany, you're welcome to come along."

"Love to," Tiffany said as she flicked her hair back with her fingers.

Swell, Emily thought. She glanced at Amanda, who rolled her eyes.

"That painting reminds me of your cousin George," Emily said to Amanda.

"Don't mention Cousin George! He's thousands of miles away and I don't want to think about him."

"You're not being fair to him. I think he's cool," Emily said, and smiled.

"I've met him once." Tiffany included herself in the conversation. "At tea with his parents and mine in London."

"I attended his birthday party," Emily volunteered, and Amanda poked her.

"Really!" Tiffany said, raising her eyebrows. "You must be a close family friend, then."

"Really," Emily echoed.

"Emily, look over there." Amanda was pointing. "Tiffany, do you see?"

"Where?"

"There's a staircase leading to another level. If we go up, I'll bet we'll be able to see everything and everybody, but maybe we won't be seen. It's like being a secret agent!"

"Will your parents wonder where we are?" Tiffany asked.

"They're not used to looking for me every minute. Nanny is the one who does that. They're so busy they'll never notice, I'm sure."

The three girls crossed the room and casually climbed the spiral staircase leading to a small balcony. No one stopped them or even seemed to notice.

"It's just another exhibit area, but not for tonight's showing," Amanda said. "We can look down and watch the adults. Do you see anything interesting?"

They peered over the edge of the polished wooden railing.

"Oh, look! That man has spilled his drink on the back of that woman's dress, but she doesn't know it." Amanda giggled and clapped a hand over her mouth.

"Where? Oh, I see! I bet the expression on the woman's face won't be a happy one when she discovers the stain!" Emily giggled. "Look at that! Over there, in the corner—a portrait of a fat man in a tuxedo, and there's the real person in a tuxedo right next to it! It couldn't be a look-alike," she said. "It must be the same guy."

Tiffany lowered her voice and asked Emily, "How did you happen to manage a weekend with the Princess? My mother's been trying to arrange for me to visit the Powers Court family for years."

Emily looked at her.

"I mean," Tiffany continued, "I don't know who you are. Your parents aren't part of the crowd, you know what I mean?"

Emily stared at Tiffany as if she had two heads.

Tiffany looked Emily up and down. "Did you win some look-alike contest?"

Emily was about to explode when Amanda leaned close and repeated a question Emily hadn't heard the first time.

"It is, isn't it?" Amanda asked.

"It's that woman!" Emily agreed. "From last night at the restaurant!"

"She's got a different feather hat on," Amanda said. "This one's yellow!"

"The same two men are with her!" Emily said. "What are they doing?" Emily leaned over the railing, but Amanda pulled her back quickly.

"Be careful! Remember, we don't want to be seen," she whispered.

But Emily was already whispering excitedly again. "Amanda, they aren't the same two men we saw last night. Well, one of them is—

the one with the slicked-back hair. But the other one isn't the same."

"What do you suppose that means?"

Tiffany Potter pushed against the railing next to them. "Who are you looking at? Oh, that woman with the ridiculous feather hat and the wavy hair? I know who she is."

"You do?" Emily and Amanda turned.

"Well, I mean, I don't actually *know* her," Tiffany said.

"Oh." The girls turned away.

"But I've seen her! Plenty of times," Tiffany said.

"We've seen her, too," Emily said.

"I mean I've seen her at all the parties my parents attend. Usually that lady wears some kind of feather boa or hat. Once she had a feathery purse."

"Do you know her name?" Amanda asked. "Is it odd or funny?"

"She goes to everyone's parties, but I don't remember her name. One can't know *every-*

one," Tiffany sniffed. "I do know all the people who count, though."

"Look at her," Amanda said. "She's as bold as a peacock."

"Mother says that type is a social climber," Tiffany repeated in her mother's voice.

"Nobody is stopping to talk to her," Amanda commented. "Should we feel sorry for her? I would. I do. I feel sorry for her. She must be lonely."

Emily sighed. "I guess adults don't always have a picnic at parties, either."

"Maybe that woman down there"— Amanda peered over the railing—"maybe she just wants to feel she belongs, and even though she keeps coming, she never fits in."

"Maybe she's just social climbing," Tiffany repeated. "Maybe she is someone who *doesn't* belong here. Maybe that's why she isn't being included."

"Maybe she should lose those dumb feather hats," Emily suggested.

Chapter Six

Emily leaned against the plush backseat of the limousine and closed her eyes for a moment.

Jack was taking the girls back to the hotel to have dinner with Nanny before he drove the Prince and Princess to their dinner party.

"I noticed you were kind enough to spend time with Tiffany Potter," Amanda's mother said. "Attractive child, isn't she?"

"Does Mrs. Potter always bring Tiffany along?" Amanda asked her mother.

"No, darling. Mrs. Potter has pledged a generous amount toward the fund. She's thoroughly American, but she understands what the contribution she makes will do for the gallery. Speaking of Americans, Emily, dear!" the Princess said suddenly.

"Yes, ma'am," Emily answered, surprised at being spoken to directly.

"There was much discussion about the benefit tomorrow night at Carnegie Hall. It seems everyone we saw just now at the gallery is going to be there. Don't your parents have something to do with this event?"

"Yes, they're artists' representatives, ma'am. They organized the show."

"Show business people will be there, is that correct?"

"People in the music business is probably a better way to say it, ma'am."

"The program is to raise funds for homeless people—" She turned to the Prince. "Isn't that what Margaret Mayfield said?"

The Prince nodded.

"Yes, ma'am, it's a benefit, and the money will be used to help homeless people," Emily said. "Especially children."

"When your mother rang up, I was in such a rush to get ready for this evening, I suppose I didn't catch all the information. That's a terribly worthwhile cause."

Emily looked at Amanda, who looked back at Emily, a tiny smile curling the corners of her mouth.

"We had something else scheduled for tomorrow evening, but perhaps we can . . . What time did you say it began, Emily?"

Emily, who hadn't said, thought a minute. She knew she would be attending, which meant she had to leave Amanda at . . . What time had her mother told her she'd come pick Emily up?

"Eight o'clock, ma'am," Jack said from the driver's seat. "We'd arranged for me to bring Miss Emily to meet her parents at the stage door at seven-thirty tomorrow evening."

"Mummy, do you think you and Daddy and I might be able to go after all?" Amanda asked hopefully.

The Princess glanced at the Prince. He smiled at his daughter. "We'll see, my dear," he answered.

"We're at the hotel already," Amanda's mother said. "Now, you have a lovely dinner with Nanny, my darling. . . ."

The hotel doorman opened their car door, and Megan, the lady-in-waiting, came out to accompany the girls up to their suite.

The lower part of Nanny's leg was in a large cast, and it was propped up on a pile of down pillows in the middle of the bed. She was wearing a bedjacket of pale pink, topped with a round lace collar. Her hair, as usual, was pulled back into a severe bun.

"How are you feeling, Nanny?" Amanda drew a chair next to the bed.

"I suppose I'm as well as can be expected,"

Nanny said primly. "Nothing for it, after all . . ."

"We've missed you," Amanda said dutifully.

"What *have* you been doing without me? Has Megan chosen the correct clothes for you? Have you been cleaning your teeth, eating your vegetables? I'm sure you have remembered your manners when meeting new people, but I hope you've not given your mother any sulky moments."

"I'm fine, truly. And Emily's here. We've come to have our dinner with you. Megan will have it brought to us right here. Won't that be nice?"

When they had finished their dinner, Nanny announced that she was tired. Emily and Amanda left her and went into their room, where they bounced on the huge fluffy duvets and talked.

"This is what it's like when you have someone sleep at your house overnight, isn't it?" Amanda asked happily.

Emily looked around the fancy hotel room. "Well . . . not exactly like *this,*" she answered.

"Oh, you know what I mean. Two friends . . . left on their own . . . talking, laughing. . . . What else do you do?"

"Sometimes we gossip or tell scary stories."

"Gossip? About what?"

"Other people. Girls in school. Boys. Teachers."

"I hate gossip. Reporters pry and write about our family. So much of it is nasty and untrue. Do you do that?"

Emily thought for a minute. "Sometimes we do say awful things. Things a princess wouldn't say. But we never print it in a newspaper. It's secrets between friends."

"Like *what*?"

"Oh, that one's stuck-up, this one's got big ears, do you think he likes me . . . that sort of thing."

"I guess I wouldn't say those sorts of things."

"See? Told you."

"But only because I've no one to say them to!"

Emily laughed. "Sorry," she said. "I guess it's not really funny. It must be hard to be alone so much of the time."

"Oh, I'm not alone. I have Nanny."

"I don't mean *that*," Emily said.

"I know. And I do have cousins. . . . But, you know, it's always arranged, planned. A party, a tea, some games. I never know if the friendship is genuine."

"Tiffany Potter would love to be your friend. I bet your parents would like her, too. Her parents aren't in show business, I don't think."

"Emily!" Amanda's eyes were wide.

Emily hung her head. "I'm sorry, Amanda. Actually, I do know what you mean about genuine friends. People who don't disappoint you. At school there are kids who want to be my friend because my parents know some big rock stars. The kids could care less about me. I hate being used."

Amanda said quietly, "Do you think my parents are snobs, Emily?"

Emily looked up. "Your parents are in a special category, Amanda," she said. "They're expected to behave a certain way. But someone like Tiffany Potter, who is from New York City, just like me, isn't special. Rich doesn't make you special. Besides, your parents invited me to stay with you, didn't they? I'm definitely not special. My parents know a lot of famous people, but we're not rich as far as I can tell!"

Amanda cleared her throat. "What else do you do when you have sleepovers?"

"We might watch TV or try on my mother's makeup and perfume, fix each other's hair. Probably we'd order a pizza."

"Oh, smashing! Let's do that!"

"What?"

"All of it!" Amanda cried. "We could use Mummy's makeup, and she has *wonderful* perfume! It's made in Grasse, in France. If we fix each other's hair, it will be like doing our own. Our hair is practically identical! We must order a pizza from room service!"

Emily was laughing. "But we've just eaten a huge meal!"

"I don't care, do you? I'm in America with my American friend and I want to do everything I'd do if I were at your house. I'll never have another chance to do any of these things again! I wouldn't be doing them now if Nanny weren't— Oh, I didn't mean that I'm *glad* about Nanny."

"Come on, *you* call for the pizza. Room service will expect to hear an English accent coming from this suite!"

Between them, they managed to finish the whole pizza.

"Do you think we'll be sick?" Amanda asked, rubbing her tummy.

"Well, when I smell tomato sauce *and* French perfume, I would say it's possible." Emily lay back on the floor and groaned.

"Let's control ourselves. It would spoil everything," Amanda said.

"Okay, Princess, whatever you say."

"Try taking deep breaths," Amanda said. "Mummy always takes deep breaths to stay calm."

"I am *so* full. And tired. How about you?" Emily asked.

"Mmm, me too. Emily? Did it sound to you as if Mummy was thinking of changing her mind about tomorrow night after all?"

Emily thought back to the limousine ride home. "Maybe," she said.

"I want to see the Mashed Potatoes so badly. I just *love* them! They're simply smashing!"

"Everybody loves them now. You know where their latest album is on the charts this week?"

"Do you?"

"I have to know! They're right at the top! They're very hot, those Mashed Potatoes."

"I almost don't care, but tell me, who else will be playing?"

"The program includes music from the twenties up to now—and some opera, too! The point is to make the audience happy, to find something every single person likes."

"That makes sense. If you're happy, I suppose you're more likely to feel charitable."

"Right."

"I do hope Mummy has decided to go, though. Daddy will go along, I know it."

"I hope so, too. What happens tomorrow during our whole day together? I can't believe I have to go back to school on Monday!"

"I don't have the slightest idea," Amanda answered. "I'd love to spend more time exploring New York City. But I'm usually just cleaned up and dressed, and I'm to follow the schedule graciously."

"Sounds like some kind of princess."

"Pre-cisely."

Chapter Seven

"A brunch! Lovely! We're going to a brunch, Emily!" Amanda turned to Emily, and when she was sure her mother couldn't see her face, she crossed her eyes.

Emily bit her lip to keep from laughing. "Nice!" was her comment.

"Yes, it's at noon," the Princess said, checking her hair in a wall mirror. "By the way, Emily, dear?"

"Yes, ma'am?"

"I do believe we shall be attending tonight's performance after all."

"Really!" Amanda cried, then instantly quieted down. "Excuse me, Mummy," she whispered.

The Princess ignored her outburst. "After all, the reason for bringing you along, Amanda, was so that we could spend more time together, isn't that right? And I know how keen you are to see this, ah, program."

"Thank you, Mummy."

"Why don't you ring your parents, Emily, and tell them we accept their kind invitation," the Princess said, nodding toward the telephone on a small end table.

Emily held the phone receiver to her ear. "Yes, Mom. Her Lady—I mean Her Princessness—uh, Amanda's mother says they can all come to the benefit after all. . . . Yes, they worked it into their, uh, *shed-ule*. What? *You'll* pick us up? Forget it, Mom. We all won't fit into our car. Jack will bring us in the limo and

91

we'll meet you. What do you mean, you'll hire a limo for everybody? You *will*?" Emily put her hand over the mouthpiece and looked up at the Princess, who was still idly playing with her hair in front of the mirror.

"Ma'am? My mom says—"

"Thank her awfully, dear, but there's no need for her to put herself out. Jack will take us all."

Emily spoke into the phone again. "It's okay, Mom, the—I mean, Amanda's mother—says Jack will take us."

"I know, Mummy!" Amanda piped up. "Why doesn't Jack take the two of us, Emily and me, and Emily's mummy and daddy can take you. Emily and I would so like to be on our own for just a little while!"

"That makes sense, ma'am," Emily added politely. "After the concert I'll go home with my parents in their car, and Jack will be there to drive you and Amanda and, uh, Amanda's father back here to the hotel."

The Princess blotted her lipstick on a small piece of tissue and stared at the result in the mirror. "Mmm, all right, yes, I suppose that will do," she said. Emily didn't know whether she was talking about her lipstick or the travel arrangements.

"Mummy?" Amanda asked.

"Ma'am?" Emily asked at the same time.

"Excuse me? Oh, yes, fine. Ask her to meet us here at the hotel."

"She says that's okay, Mom," Emily said into the phone. "We'll go with Jack in their car, and you come here to pick up Amanda's parents. No, Mom, I'm not kidding," Emily whispered. "It's really okay! Good, see you later, bye." She hung up and looked across the room at Amanda, who was beaming.

"What will we do until noon?" Emily asked. "It's only nine-thirty! I'm hungry!"

"How can you be hungry," Amanda said, "after last night? I'm still so full!"

"I don't know. I'm always hungry after I sleep."

"Well," Amanda said, "we could ring up room service and order something if you'd like."

Emily thought. "Wait," she said, "I've got a better idea! Do you think Jack could go with us for a while?"

"I don't see why not. He's not doing anything until he has to drive us all to the brunch. What's your idea?"

They walked down Fifth Avenue until they came to an entrance to the park. The first thing they did was buy three enormous hot-dogs-with-everything from a vendor.

"Oh, Emily! So *this* is Central Park!" Amanda exclaimed as she munched the hot dog. "I caught a glimpse of it yesterday when we were coming out of the museum, but I never thought I'd get to walk in it!"

"It's eight hundred and forty-three acres,"

Jack announced. "It's bounded on the north by One Hundred Tenth Street and on the south by Fifty-ninth Street. The east border is Fifth Avenue, which we've just been walking on, and the west border is Central Park West."

"Thank you, Jack."

"You're welcome."

"What are we going to do here?" Amanda asked.

"Oh, there's *tons* of things to do in the park," Emily said, "but what I wanted us to do is throw a Frisbee around."

"A Frisbee?"

"Yeah, you'll see. Let's walk a little bit."

Together they walked along the path. Jack still held tight to the girls' hands.

"Don't worry, Jack," Emily said, looking up at him. "We're perfectly safe."

"I've heard stories about the park, Miss Emily," he said warily. "It's supposed to be rather dangerous."

Emily nodded. "You don't want to come

here alone at night, that's true," she said. "But on a bright Sunday morning like this one— Look at all the people! Moms and kids, dog walkers, bikers, joggers, kite flyers, boyfriends and girlfriends . . ." And homeless families, Emily started to say, but thought better of it. Amanda looked so delighted with everything, she didn't want to spoil it for her friend. Besides, Amanda and her family would hear a lot about some of these families tonight. "Anyway," Emily went on, "there's a wonderful zoo just a few blocks up." She pointed.

"I'd feel better if you stayed close to me, young ladies," Jack said.

They bought a Frisbee and found an open space. "This is how you do it," Emily explained. "Jack, go over there. No, farther! Just a little farther, Jack? You can still see us. . . . Great! Now watch!"

She whizzed the Frisbee at him, watching his face as it glided toward him. He caught it easily, laughing, and tossed it back.

"Oh, I want to have a go!" Amanda said, and Emily threw the Frisbee in her direction.

Amanda, a natural athlete, had taken lessons in everything from ballet to swimming, from horseback riding to tennis.

"Emily! Catch!" she called, and hurled the Frisbee toward her friend.

"Got it! I got it!" Emily cried, and jumped high in the air, stretching out her arm.

But the Frisbee sailed past her, and she turned quickly so as not to lose sight of it.

It was caught by a grinning boy who laughed as he sent it whirling toward Jack, who caught it reflexively.

"You're the boy from yesterday!" Emily cried.

Jack hurried to Amanda and stepped in front of her. "From the ferry?" he asked Emily. "The one you saw watching you on the boat?"

Emily nodded.

"Hi," the boy called as he sauntered over to them.

"Young man, who are you?" Jack inquired in a voice that sounded menacing.

"Eddie," the boy answered casually. "You their father?" He stuck his chin out at Jack.

"Pardon?" Jack asked incredulously.

"You their father?" Eddie repeated more loudly, as if Jack might be hard of hearing. "The *twins*!" He pointed to Emily and Amanda and spoke slowly. "Are the twins your daughters?"

Amanda burst out laughing.

"It's no coincidence you're here, is it, Eddie?" Jack asked. He didn't answer Eddie's question. He didn't look at all amused.

"No, sir, it's not. I saw you yesterday on the ferry to Ellis. I ride it all the time."

"All the time?" Emily asked, her eyes wide.

"Yep. And I thought you were—hey, you know . . . I liked watching you." He looked up at Jack, who was glaring at him. "But I didn't mean any harm—really! The twins here—I mean, you know, they—"

"They what?" Jack asked.

Eddie took a deep breath. "They're—you know, they're so pretty. They looked so nice. You were standing over them like you were protecting them with your life. I just wanted to find out about you."

"Would you kindly explain yourself?"

"Sometimes I find someone on the ferry that I'd like to—I mean, that I wished I was—ah, never mind." He turned to walk away, but Amanda gently held up her hand for him to stay.

"You wish what?" she asked. "What do you do with the people on the ferry?"

The boy turned, but he didn't look at her.

"I don't do anything against the law. Really. I—I follow people home, sometimes. See where they live. Figure out what their lives are like." He looked at Jack again. "But I don't hurt anyone or steal. I swear!"

Jack still stood blocking Amanda. He asked, "Where do you live?"

As Eddie looked at the smartly dressed, attractive redheaded girls and the tall, protective man with them, he realized he'd talked too much. "Listen, I'm outta here. Sorry I bothered you. So long."

"Eddie, how old are you?" Emily piped up.

"Fifteen," he answered quickly.

"Fifteen?" Jack asked.

"Well, thirteen, almost fourteen."

Amanda stepped from behind Jack and asked softly, "Where do you live?"

Eddie cleared his throat and looked around. "Nowhere near here. I mean, not where you'd—"

Emily looked at Eddie and then took two steps closer to him. "Eddie? Do you even have a home?" she asked kindly.

He didn't answer.

"Oh, wow," Emily whispered. Amanda looked puzzled, and Jack seemed ready to herd the girls back toward the car.

Eddie suddenly turned and began to walk away. Just as suddenly, he turned back. "My family hangs out under the George Washington Bridge," he called out defensively. "There's a bunch of us . . ." He looked at their expressions. "Don't feel sorry for me," he said. "We'll be okay. My family's had some bad luck. I do all right. I ride the ferry to the Statue of Liberty and Ellis a lot. People pay for me. You know . . . when they hear how I'm an immigrant and all."

"Are you?" Amanda asked. "An immigrant?"

He blushed. "Nah . . . born right here, in NYC."

Amanda whispered to Jack, "He's probably hungry! We must do something!"

Jack looked at her and ever so slightly shook his head.

"Where are your parents?" Emily asked. Eddie just shrugged and looked away. His chin was jutting out. Emily thought he was probably getting angry with them. After all, he didn't mean any harm, and here they were, butting into his life.

He shoved his hands into the deep pockets of his oversized corduroy jacket.

"We're not being nosy. Honest," Emily said. "We're interested in you, that's all. After all, you *did* follow us, right? I mean, we didn't follow you."

"I guess," he said. He sighed, then said, "Never knew my father, mother took off with her boyfriend. End of story."

"Listen," Emily said. "Maybe there's a really good reason we all met. There's a benefit tonight to raise money. It's to help the—it's for people who don't have homes."

"You mean money for soup kitchens, shelters, stuff like that," Eddie said.

"Well, for clothes and medical care," Emily said quickly. "My parents are involved with the benefit. Maybe you should come. You could help people who don't really understand the situation, by talking about what you need to survive."

Eddie shifted his feet. "A bunch of do-gooders like that never really want to understand," he said. "I know you probably mean to do a good thing, but—"

Jack and Amanda stared at Eddie and then at Emily.

"Look, don't get me wrong," Emily said. "Go get something to eat now, why don't you." She handed Eddie the few bills she had in her wallet. "Don't be embarrassed. Please, just come to the stage door of Carnegie Hall tonight at eight o'clock. You know where Carnegie Hall is?"

"I may be poor and homeless, but I'm not

dumb," Eddie said proudly. "I know where every place in New York is. I could be a taxi driver or a tour guide!"

"Miss Emily," Jack said, beckoning to her.

Emily went to Jack, getting ready to convince him that her idea was okay.

"I believe he ought to come earlier than eight," Jack said, and smiled.

"You're right. And you're great, Jack. We're doing the right thing," Emily said.

"Yes," Amanda put in, "but perhaps we could, ah, how shall I put it?" She whispered to Emily, "Might it be possible to get him a shower, you know, perhaps some proper clothes?"

"Right! Oh, you're right." Emily clapped her hands. "We'll get him stuff from Wardrobe! And there are plenty of places for him to clean up backstage."

Amanda turned to Eddie and smiled as Emily said, "How about something new to wear to the show?"

He grinned a lopsided grin.

"Seven," she said. "Be there at seven."

"Uh—one thing," he said, stuffing his hands in his pockets again.

"What?"

"What're your names?" he asked finally. "I mean, I should know your names. If you're paying for me. So if someone stops me, in case you change your mind or something."

"Oh, we've been dreadfully rude," Amanda said.

"She's Amanda," Emily said, "I'm Emily, and this is Jack. We won't change our plans. You can count on us."

They shook hands stiffly all around.

"Okay," Eddie said. "So you're twins, right? And you're the dad?"

"Well, not exactly. We're friends," Amanda explained, "and Jack is our—"

"Baby-sitter!" Emily finished.

Eddie pointed to each girl. "So you're not even related?" He shook his head.

"We're just good friends," Emily answered. "You coulda fooled me," Eddie said. "Except you two"—he pointed at Amanda and Jack—"talk funny. You've got different accents. Here's what I pictured: You guys were probably a divorced family with—with the dad now reunited with both of you girls." He smiled at them. "I like happy endings. All my made-up stories end with them." He laughed and turned away. "See you later," he called with a wave.

As they walked back to the hotel, Amanda was thoughtful. "Imagine, no parents *and* no place to live at all."

"I guess it's really hard for you to imagine something that awful," Emily said. "I mean, it's not something *you* see at all. I do. I mean, this benefit my parents are producing—I know the homeless are real. I see them on my way to school, here in the city, on subway trains, in doorways. I mean, I have a nice house and food and clothes and everything, but I still see the people who don't."

"I know they're real, too," Amanda said, "but I don't see them. My world is so different. I know you said the benefit was for homeless people, but I was really just keen to see the Mashed Potatoes again."

"It's not your fault, Amanda," Emily said. "When you're born into such a special world, it's hard to imagine that there are people who have nothing. Your parents must think *I'm* poor!"

"Miss Emily, will it be all right with your parents that you've invited this young man?" Jack asked.

"It will be just fine with them," Emily said.

"Eddie followed us yesterday," Amanda mused. "He saw where we're staying in that elegant hotel. He wanted to be like us."

"He probably wanted to pretend he had a great life," Emily said. "That's why he fol- lowed us to the park. I just wanted you to have some American-type fun, Amanda—play Frisbee and stuff. I didn't think we'd meet someone like Eddie."

"It *was* fun," Amanda said. Then she added slowly, "Eddie can go to the park and play, but he doesn't get to go home to a nice warm place and have lunch or tea or dinner and have people looking after him, the way we do. Perhaps . . . perhaps we shouldn't be having fun after all."

"Now that you've met Eddie, Miss Amanda, it doesn't mean you're not to enjoy yourself anymore," Jack said in a kind voice. "It doesn't mean that at all. It means only that now you know there's another side of things to think about. Those who have been blessed must give something back."

"That's what my parents always say," Emily said. "That's why we'll all have a great time at the benefit tonight."

Chapter Eight

The brunch was being held at the home of Mr. and Mrs. Lloyd Ditherfield. Madge Ditherfield had been a close friend of the Powers Court family for decades—in fact, she was a distant cousin. The Princess of Powers Court always enjoyed her chats with Madge because they disliked the same relatives. They gossiped together and never worried what the other might think. The Princess could also count on the Ditherfields to make a substantial contribution to the fund to replace the roof of the National Portrait Gallery.

"We *knew* you'd both be here!" Mrs. Potter

gushed at Emily and Amanda as the girls entered with the Prince and Princess. "Tiffany couldn't bear the thought of missing you, she *so* enjoyed you both at the gallery yesterday evening!"

Tiffany, curling a strand of her long blond hair around her finger, smiled from behind her mother.

"She was invited to a classmate's birthday brunch at a wonderful private club this afternoon, weren't you, Tiffany darling, but she said she'd rather be here at the Ditherfields' since *you* would be here. Didn't you, dear?"

"Yes, Mother," Tiffany replied. "Even though Brittany was going to be giving out handmade gifts."

"Sorry you missed the party," Emily said. "Is it too late to change your mind?"

"It's nice that you're here," Amanda said quickly.

"Thank you," Tiffany answered.

Emily gently elbowed Amanda. "Look!" she whispered.

"I see!" Amanda answered.

"What?" Tiffany asked.

Emily glowered at her.

"Well?" Tiffany asked.

Emily tilted her chin in the direction of the drawing room door.

"Oh! I see!" Tiffany exclaimed.

"What color would you call the feather in her hat this time?" Amanda asked with a small smile.

"Kelly green," Emily said softly.

"Let's go over there and see if we can get some news about who she is and what she's saying."

"Why do you care what she's saying?" Tiffany asked, but the girls didn't answer. They began to make their way through the throng of guests.

"There's her regular friend, the guy with the slicked-back hair," Emily said, "but there's a new guy, too. The *second* new guy. What do you make of that?"

"What are you two doing?" Tiffany asked. "Are you playing a game? Detective or something? Don't you think, if you'll pardon me, Princess, that that's for kids?"

Amanda smiled but didn't answer.

The girls stood beside the food table nearest the woman and listened.

"Isn't that our hostess?" the woman asked, and her feathered head bounced around.

"It sure is," said the man with slicked-back hair.

"Look at her hairdo! It went out in the twenties! Some people have no style."

"Never mind the hairdo. Check out what she's got around her neck! That's the genuine article."

Amanda and Emily both turned slightly to locate Mrs. Ditherfield.

"Which one is Mrs. Ditherfield?" Emily whispered.

Amanda signaled with her eyes toward a plump blond woman in purple silk. "She's a very nice person. Mummy likes her."

"I know Mrs. Ditherfield," Tiffany said. "I call her Aunt Madge. She's practically a member of my family!"

Amanda held a finger to her lips.

"I don't get it." Tiffany munched on a stick of celery. "Why do you two care what those tacky old toads are saying?"

"Shhh!" Emily hissed.

"Quite striking, that necklace," the feathery woman was saying. "It looks heavy."

"It oughta be," said the man. "It's worth a fortune."

"Diamonds and sapphires," said the new man. "An exquisite combination."

"Are you sure it's not fake?" asked the woman.

"I'm sure," said the man. "That's why you brought me in, because I know by just looking."

"Right. Sorry, Ed. Of course she'd have the authentic piece."

Tiffany Potter was bored. She'd missed her classmate's brunch because her mother wanted her to befriend Princess Amanda of Powers Court, but the Princess wasn't really fun and her American friend was a nobody. Now she had to stand around listening to the people at the party with the *worst* clothes, and she hadn't the least idea why!

"Why don't I tell you about the best stores for shopping?" she suggested. "I know them *all*! What are you looking for—riding clothes, jewelry, shoes? Of course you have shops in London, but New York boutiques are so— Ow!"

"Oh, sorry, I stepped on your foot by accident," Emily said. "It sure is crowded in here."

Tiffany glowered.

Amanda moved to Emily's right and tried to tune in on the trio's conversation.

"Look, see that woman over there?" the man asked. "In the green suit?"

"The one reaching for the champagne glass?"

"Exactly. She's wearing a brooch on her shoulder, see it?"

"Emeralds! Aren't they lovely! That's a look."

"Paste, Marjorie. Only paste. Worth a thousand at the most. A good copy, but the sparkle tells all."

"No kidding!"

"Now she's probably got the real one at home in a safe, and who can blame her when the likes of us are out and about?"

"It's the Ditherfield woman I'm interested in. That's the necklace I can place for a fortune. Queen Victoria's sapphires and diamonds! The people who want it won't ask questions. They'll just add to their collection! Let's move around before we start looking too obvious."

The conversation among the three stopped.

"Your Highness?" Tiffany asked Amanda. When she heard those two words, Amanda's face suddenly turned white.

"I'm fine, Tiffany. Oh, there's Mummy!" Amanda said loudly, taking Emily's arm. "Let's go see her! Come along, Tiffany."

Emily peered at Mrs. Ditherfield as they passed among her guests. "That necklace is unreal," Emily commented.

"It's *magnificent*. They *are* Queen Victoria's sapphires and diamonds! Mummy owns the matching earrings!" Amanda whispered. "Mrs. Ditherfield is a cousin of ours, you know. She married an American. And she and Mr. Ditherfield managed to buy Queen Victoria's necklace!"

"What!" Emily cried.

"It's true!"

"I can't hear either of you with all these grown-ups talking," Tiffany said. "I'm going to get a soda."

"Well, if it was Queen Victoria's, I guess you'd know . . . ," Emily said to Amanda.

"Those three are thieves, Emily!" Amanda whispered. "That's why they've been turning up at all the parties. The lady with the feather must be the connection to the posh, proper people. She brings some man each time who knows what to look for! Nanny has read me enough Sherlock Holmes stories that I know what's afoot."

"Whoa," Emily breathed. "It has to be, even if we *are* just kids. I think you figured it out!" Her eyes widened.

"I'll wager they're responsible for the jewel theft everyone's talking about!" Amanda said.

"Why weren't they afraid to be here?" Emily asked. "We could hear everything they said!"

"That's because we were *trying* to listen! Emily, you know how these parties are. No one ever listens to anyone. Besides, don't forget, we're just children. We never understand

anything grown-ups say. We're always ignored, we never count, do we?" She grinned
at her friend.

"I'm back!" Suddenly Tiffany popped up
beside them. "I hope you didn't miss me too
much," she added with a sour smile.

"Welcome back," Emily said. "You're just
in time to eat."

The brunch was served buffet-style in the
Ditherfields' beautiful dining room. Emily
thought of Eddie and kids like him, who probably couldn't even imagine this much food.
She almost felt guilty. She didn't know what
to take first. Her upbringing reminded her not
to grab, but her stomach wanted it all!

Tiffany didn't seem bothered by etiquette,
Emily noticed. She was eating everything in
sight.

Emily watched Amanda: A little of this, a
little of that. . . . No, thank you, not
that. . . .

Emily sighed. Amanda *ate* like a princess, too.

"Aren't you hungry?" she asked while Tiffany was helping herself to more rolls.

"Starved!" Amanda answered.

"But look at your plate! I could roll marbles around on it and never hit anything!"

"Emily, when I finish this, I will go back to the table."

"And back? And back? And back again?"

"Exactly! But I won't look like a little pig if anyone happens to be watching."

"After what we just heard, I probably should have lost my appetite. In the movies, I never see detectives eating."

"When you're all excited or upset about something, you just want to eat," Amanda said matter-of-factly.

"And here's Princess Amanda! My, you're lovelier than ever, my sweet. You are growing up into a fine young lady, I can see that."

Amanda put her plate down on the table

and held out her hand. "Lovely to see you again, Mrs. Ditherfield," she said, shaking hands with the woman. "What a marvelous brunch! My parents and I were so thrilled that we would be seeing you during our visit to New York."

"It's a pleasure, Princess."

"Mrs. Ditherfield, may I present my friend Emily Chornak? Emily, this is Mrs. Ditherfield, our hostess."

"How do you do, Mrs. Ditherfield?" Emily said politely.

"Chornak? Why, you must be Helen and Daniel's daughter," Mrs. Ditherfield said. "I haven't seen your parents since that wonderful concert for the diabetes foundation."

"Yes, ma'am," Emily replied sweetly.

"Why, how nice that you and Princess Amanda are friends! We'll be seeing your parents tonight, of course. Everyone wants to be there!" Mrs. Ditherfield smiled.

"Where?" Tiffany asked. "Where exactly?" Her voice came out squeaky with excitement.

"Why, the benefit for the homeless at Carnegie Hall, of course!" Mrs. Ditherfield exclaimed. "Young Emily's parents are producing it, Tiffany."

Tiffany looked startled. She suddenly smiled a winning smile at Emily.

Emily nodded at Mrs. Ditherfield. "I'm glad you'll be there. It's a worthy cause."

"Wouldn't miss it! And how nice that the Prince and Princess will be able to attend. Nice to have met you, Emily, dear," Mrs. Ditherfield said. "Give my love to your darling mother. I'm so looking forward to this evening! Tiffany, why don't you come with me for a moment. I don't think your uncle Lloyd has seen you this afternoon!"

Emily watched Mrs. Ditherfield move away, holding Tiffany's hand. Then Emily moved closer to Amanda. "You didn't say anything to her about the guests who want her neck-lace."

"Well, neither did you," Amanda said.

"Can you just imagine her face if I said something like, 'See those three people over there? Tonight they're going to break into this place and find your safe or wherever you hide your jewels and make away with that cute lit-tle sparkly thing around your neck!' "

Amanda smiled. "I might have chosen dif-ferent words, but she wouldn't have believed me, either."

"But you're Princess Amanda of Powers Court!"

"I'm also not quite eleven years old."

"Right." Emily sighed. "I should get real. They'd say we've got overactive imaginations and think we'd been sneaking cups of the champagne punch! I guess the police won't be-lieve us, either. Will your parents, if you call and tell them?"

"Would yours?"

"Don't be silly. I can hardly believe it my-self."

Amanda tried to think of someone who might listen to them. "We could tell Nanny exactly what we heard," she said. "But she'd just get herself into a big bother and keep me in the hotel thinking I was running a fever."

"I don't know what we should do," Emily said.

"I haven't a clue either," Amanda said. "Just keep thinking."

"I just adore Madge Ditherfield, don't you, darling?" the Princess was saying as they drove back to the hotel. "Even if she did manage to get her hands on that sapphire-and-diamond necklace we should have had when we acquired the earrings."

Amanda's and Emily's eyes met, but they said nothing.

"Lovely brunch, wasn't it?" the Princess said.

The Prince smiled.

"Yes, I thought so, too," the Princess answered herself. "And did you see dear Carolyn? She's been ill, poor thing, that's why we haven't seen her at any of the parties. How do you think she looked?"

Amanda asked softly, "Mummy?"

"Yes, darling?" her mother answered as she looked out the window of the limousine.

"There was a rather oddly dressed woman at the brunch party this afternoon. She wears a sort of rhinestone cap with a colored feather. Did you notice her?" Amanda and Emily exchanged glances again.

"Let me see," the Princess said. "Blond? Quite glittery and rather vulgar in appearance?"

"That's the one!" Amanda said excitedly. "Do you know her?"

"Why, no. I certainly wouldn't care to, either. I assume she's a friend of a friend of someone's. After all, how else would she have been invited?"

"But, Mummy, you were never introduced?"

The Princess frowned. "Why, no, I don't believe we were. I do remember her, though— so conspicuous. I mean, those ridiculous feathers! Why do you need to know about her, dear? I'd prefer you stay well away from her sort."

"Yes, Mummy. We were just curious because her clothes are so awful."

Once back at the hotel, Amanda and Emily looked in on Nanny.

"She's on the mend," Amanda observed as they left Nanny's room.

"Well, sure, she's discovered the wonders of the remote control!" Emily laughed. "Did you see her zapping away? I think she's becoming very American!"

"Well, I'm glad she's feeling better," Amanda said. "I didn't feel quite truthful not telling her about Eddie or even mentioning our idea about the burglary. I didn't lie, of course, but I didn't tell her what happened. I don't want to make her fuss or worry her, after all. I suppose we should do what she suggested, don't you?"

"Take a nap until it's time to get ready? How can we sleep, knowing what we know?"

Chapter Nine

Both girls fell asleep the moment their heads touched their pillows. They had to be awakened by Megan. She served them something to eat before the show.

As they were getting dressed, Emily admitted, "I feel better."

Amanda nodded. "So do I. Now we must think about what to do next. We can't stand idly by and allow a theft to happen, if it's really being planned. I think the one adult who might listen to us is Jack, but I'm not sure we have enough evidence so that he won't think we're completely off our heads."

"We'll just have to try," Emily answered.

"There's no one else we can turn to without looking like total idiots."

Promptly at six-forty-five, Jack appeared to escort the girls from their suite to the car.

"Jack, we have urgent business to discuss," Amanda said at once. "You must promise to listen and not to simply think we're foolish little girls. Now, you must have seen this woman—"

Emily couldn't contain herself. "Jack, there was a lady wearing feathered hats, each day a different-colored one, at every event we attended. Did you see her?"

"What about this feathered friend of yours?" Jack said. "Why is she so important? What's all the bother about?"

By this time they had swooped through the lobby, dancing around Jack and jumping up and down in front of him to make sure he took note of everything they were telling him.

Now they were at the car, so they waited until he had held the door for them and taken his place in the driver's seat.

"Jack!" Amanda spoke first. "What would you do if you were at a party—"

"—and you overheard some people talking—" Emily interrupted.

"—and you could tell from the conversation that they were planning to do something awful!" Amanda finished.

"How do you mean, 'awful'?" Jack drove the car away from the curb and headed toward the West Side.

"I'll just say it outright. They were planning a robbery, a theft," Amanda said. "We were standing right next to them and they didn't even realize we heard because—"

"—because there were a lot of people talking and we're just kids, so to them we were invisible," Emily went on.

"You actually heard this, did you?" Jack asked.

131

"Actually!" they both answered. "So what would you do?"

"You haven't told anyone?" Jack asked.

"No," Emily said. "Amanda said no one would believe us, and I thought she was right. We think these must be the people who have been doing all these robberies everyone keeps talking about."

"They were discussing which jewels were real and which were paste. They said they wanted Mrs. Ditherfield's sapphire-and-diamond necklace and that they wanted it tonight! Someone wants to buy it even if it's stolen. It's worth a fortune," Amanda finished breathlessly.

"That's not a lot of real evidence, you know," Jack said.

"But Mummy and Daddy don't know this woman with the feathered cap," Amanda said.

Jack chuckled. "Your parents don't know *everyone,* you know."

"Oh, Jack, it's not just that. It's—"

"I know. It's just that even if you're right, there isn't very much to tell anyone, is there? You don't know the woman or the men, you can't prove they've nicked any jewels, and you don't know where they are now. As far as I can see, the only crime committed is that ghastly hat with the feather on it!"

The girls looked at each other and sank back in their seats. Even if anyone at all believed them, they couldn't prove anything. They didn't even know the woman's full name. Her first name was Marjorie, Amanda remembered. No help. And even if they were absolutely right and the Queen Victoria necklace was stolen from Mrs. Ditherfield that very night, there would still be no evidence to prove who had done it. "There must be something we can do," Amanda said. "We can't just let this happen." Both girls sighed deeply.

————

With Jack on her right, Amanda stood in one of the dressing rooms backstage at Carnegie Hall, waiting for Emily.

"How do I look?" Eddie asked, grinning at Amanda's expression as they came over to her.

"You look like a different person!" Amanda exclaimed.

Emily smiled and explained. "Eddie cleaned up and changed in the Mashed Potatoes' dressing room. Liza's hairdresser fixed his hair, and the wardrobe people found this suit and shoes that fit. No one will guess Eddie's homeless until he gets to tell his story."

Eddie pointed with his thumb toward Emily. "Remember, they said I could keep the clothes, too," he said.

Amanda nodded approvingly. "You look absolutely smashing, Eddie. Really!"

"My, it's filling up quite rapidly, isn't it?" Amanda's mother, the Princess, said as they filed into the fourth row in the concert hall.

"It's sold out," Emily's father told her. "We couldn't be more pleased. It's taken a lot of work to bring us to this moment."

"I'm sure. Oh, look, there's Madge, she's coming down the aisle. Look, she's waving." The Princess waved back.

Amanda swiveled around to see Mrs. Ditherfield, hoping she might be wearing the sapphire-and-diamond necklace, hoping her home was not being broken into as they all stood there, hoping—

"Emily!"

"What?"

"Guess!"

"She's here, right?"

Amanda nodded.

Eddie was shown to his seat next to Emily. "Are you looking at someone special?" he asked.

Amanda leaned over and whispered, "We think there's a jewel thief here, and we've been trying to figure out how to stop her committing her next crime."

Emily added, "We have no proof. No one would believe us."

Eddie was craning his neck. "So who we looking for? Which one? Let me check him out."

"Her, Eddie. It's a woman. Turn around, quickly," Amanda warned him. "We don't want her to think we know."

"She's usually wearing a feather," Emily whispered.

"Bright red tonight," Amanda replied. "Two rows back. Don't turn around!"

"I want to see for myself," Emily protested.

"Yeah, me too," Eddie said.

"All right, but be careful. One at a time— and don't let her see you looking!"

Emily stood as if to stretch and casually peeked behind her. "People are still being seated," she said. "Everyone's walking around, taking off their coats, talking. She won't notice us."

Eddie stood, too, and glanced around the huge auditorium.

"See the lady with the hat with the red feather?" Emily asked Eddie out of the side of her mouth.

"Got it."

"What else?" Amanda asked anxiously.

"There's a man on either side of her," Emily said. "One of them is Mr. Slick!"

"Do you recognize the other?"

"I can't be sure, but I think . . ." Emily frowned and squinted. "I think it's the same one we saw at the brunch."

Amanda frowned and started to bite her fingernail until she remembered that her mother and father were sitting right there with her. She sighed and leaned back heavily in her seat.

"Hello there!"

The Powers Courts, the Chornaks, and Eddie looked up to see Constance Potter in the aisle, clutching her daughter's hand. Tiffany was wearing another fancy dress, this one with a big bow in the back.

"Hello, Constance." The Princess nodded.

Mrs. Potter looked up and down the fourth row, even though she could see at a glance that every seat was taken.

"I see every seat is taken," she said.

"I think she wants *me* to move," Emily whispered to Amanda.

"Oh, no, she wouldn't! She's not so rude," Amanda said.

Emily shook her head. Amanda saw good in everybody, somehow. Well, except maybe her cousin George . . .

Mrs. Potter remained standing in the aisle, but the Prince was reading his program, and the Princess wasn't fazed a bit.

Mrs. Potter tried again. "Helen?"

"Oh, hello, Constance," Emily's mother said brightly. "So glad you could come."

"Yes . . ." Mrs. Potter tapped her foot impatiently. She knew the Prince and Princess, she knew the producers of this benefit, she even knew some of the stars. Besides that, she had donated *enormous* amounts of money to all of them, and *still* that American child, that *nobody,* got to sit right there among the most important people in the house. And who was that boy?

"Mo-ther . . ."

"Yes, dear."

And her Tiffany, *easily* the best dressed of the children, stood here in the aisle, of all places!

"Mother, who's that boy?" Tiffany said, tugging at her mother's sleeve.

"I don't *know*." Her mother sighed as she answered.

"He's so *cute*! I want to meet him!"

"Tiffany," her mother whispered, "I'm *trying*!" Loudly now, she coughed and said, "Yes, well, I guess I'll have to find our seats!"

Emily watched Tiffany and Mrs. Potter seat themselves on the aisle several rows back.

Aisle seats, center section, Emily thought. Those are great seats! What's Mrs. Potter so teed off about?

Beside her, Amanda whispered, "Are you checking on our possible thief?"

Emily hadn't been, but she did now.

"She's there, all right. I hope her feather's blocking Mrs. Potter's view!"

Chapter Ten

"House to half," Emily's father whispered to her mother as the houselights dimmed.

"I'm so excited. Aren't you excited, Emily?" her mother asked.

Emily *was* excited. She was thrilled that Eddie was there.

And now the houselights were out. The audience sat in darkness until a spotlight suddenly glowed against the red velvet curtain, the orchestra played a bright fanfare, and a man in a tuxedo stepped through the parted curtain center stage.

Emily's father leaned over and whispered,

"Look, Em. We got Webley Burnside to em-cee!"

Emily smiled and nodded. Webley Burnside was a famous music critic. He wrote for the biggest New York newspaper and had his own radio show. Emily thought he was a big snob. But he *was* English, and maybe he would make an impression on the visitors.

"Good evening, ladies and gentlemen," Webley Burnside began, "*and* to the Prince and Princess of Powers Court, our honored guests." He bowed deeply from the waist as he looked at their row of seats. The Prince and Princess nodded back and smiled thin smiles.

"I and your producers"—he bowed again, toward the Chornaks, but not so deeply—"are extremely delighted to welcome you here for an evening of outstanding musical treasures, beloved through the decades, and performed by the world's greatest and most cherished art-ists . . ."

Amanda, on Emily's left, grabbed her

friend's hand and squeezed it. "Check on her again. I can't turn around," she whispered.

Emily swiveled her head slowly to her left. Then she turned back to Amanda. "Still there. Staring at the stage like everyone else."

"And the men?"

"Still there."

Someone behind them hissed, "Shhh!" and they both fell silent.

From center stage, Webley Burnside had finished his welcoming speech and was introducing the first act on the program.

". . . quite a treat for some of the younger members of our audience. . . . It's reported that these chaps have caused as many young girls to faint as the Beatles did back in the sixties!"

Emily's father laughed heartily.

"And now, all the way from London, England, I'm pleased to bring you"—he stepped back toward the wings, stage right—*"the Mashed Potatoes!"*

Amanda's eyes glowed, and she clapped as hard as she could along with the rest of the audience.

"Wow," Eddie said. "This is incredible! I can't believe I'm really here!"

As she watched Amanda, Emily momentarily forgot about the woman with the feather and about Mrs. Potter and Tiffany. Emily couldn't help smiling as she recalled Amanda's excited meeting with the Mashed Potatoes when Emily's parents had signed them on as clients in London.

As the lead singer of the group sauntered downstage, he stopped and held up his hand for the audience to quiet down. "Well, look who we have here!"

Amanda gasped.

"Could it be the lovely Princess Amanda of Powers Court?"

Amanda glanced over at her parents.

"It is! It *is* Princess Amanda, chaps!" The drummer played a loud roll. "The sweetest voice in all of Britain!" Then the lead singer of the Mashed Potatoes shook his head and laughed pleasantly.

"I don't think we'd *dare* do this back home," he said, "but since we're here in the States, where everything's a little more, ah, carefree—"

The audience laughed.

"—we'd love to do our biggest hit for you with the lovely Princess Amanda, who sings it just smashingly! *'Rocket to the Moon'*!"

The audience clapped and clapped, and someone began a chant: "A-*man*-da! A-*man*-da!"

The Princess began to fan herself with her hand, and the Prince's face was almost as red as Amanda's hair, but no one was looking at them. Not even Amanda.

"Should I do it?" she whispered to Emily. "Tell me! I'm practically frozen from excitement!"

Emily, who couldn't imagine standing up

145

on a stage in front of a crowd of people waiting for her to sing, stared at her. "Do you *want*
to?" she asked.

Amanda nodded energetically.

Emily grinned. "Then do it."

Amanda jumped up so fast she startled her
parents. Before they could stop her, she headed
toward the opposite end of their row and
rushed up the steps onto the stage.

The formally dressed audience went wild,
and as they cheered and clapped and whistled,
Amanda and the group set the key for the
song.

Within instants the music blared and the
Mashed Potatoes and Princess Amanda of
Powers Court were rocketing to the moon.

After one chorus, the lead singer yelled,
"You all know this, don't you? I want to hear
a chorus from you, too! Sing for the homeless
out there, who need a break! Sing with us and
Princess Amanda! Let's have the lights, so we
can see our audience! Lights, please!" he

yelled toward the control booth, and the houselights went on.

Emily, in her seat, was caught up in the energy filling the hall. Her eyes focused on her friend's radiant face. Then suddenly Amanda's eyes were wide and her smile changed to a grimace. She searched for Emily in the audience, and their eyes met. Amanda mouthed some words and pointed at Emily.

"I can't understand." Emily shook her head again and again.

"The man!" Amanda mouthed, cupping her hands in hopes that only Emily could see. "The man is gone! One man is gone!" She tried to act it out like a game of charades.

"She says the man's gone!" Eddie whispered. "The guy with the feather woman."

Amanda nodded furiously and pointed again.

"Are you up for another, Princess?" the lead Potato was asking.

"Excuse me?"

"Another song! Do you know 'Never Leave Me'?"

"I know all your songs!" Amanda answered.

"Then let's do it! You take the solo, Princess Amanda!"

Amanda watched the feather from the stage, Emily watched Amanda, and Eddie watched them both. Neither girl paid the slightest attention to her parents. The Chornaks couldn't have been happier; Amanda's parents were on the verge of exploding but kept their cool demeanor.

" 'I'm beggin' . . . Neeee-ver leave me, honey, Neeee-ver go . . . ,' " Amanda sang, and moved about the stage, watching what was happening in the audience.

" 'Wooo-wooo, baby . . . Ne-eed you so . . .' "

The Prince covered his mouth as if to silence a cough.

" '. . . so never leave!' "

As the song came to an end, Amanda held up two fingers to Emily.

"Both guys are gone," Eddie whispered to Emily.

Emily pantomimed the woman's feather to Amanda.

Amanda nodded. "Still here," she mouthed. "The two men are gone, but the woman's—"

Emily couldn't follow what Amanda was trying to tell her. She rose to her feet and headed for the aisle, stepping on first the Princess's and then the Prince's shoes.

Emily looked again at Amanda, who was pointing and gesturing frantically.

Emily was at the edge of the stage now, and suddenly Amanda sang out, as if she were improvising a line of the song, "She's leaving, too! She's leaving. Don't let her go-o-o. . . ."

As the words filled the hall, Mrs. Potter elbowed Tiffany in the ribs.

"Look, Tiffany, that Emily girl has left her

seat, and Princess Amanda is waving at you. I think she wants you to sit in that row now."

Tiffany raised an eyebrow.

"Yes, look, love, look how she's gesturing. Right at you, can't you tell?"

The woman with the feather had left her seat and was slowly moving toward the aisle.

"Are you sure, Mother?" Tiffany asked. "Isn't she waving at Emily?"

"No! Can't you see? She's looking *past* Emily! Into the audience! Right at you!"

Tiffany wanted to believe it. That cute boy in their row was on his feet and seemed to be looking at her, too! In fact—oh, my, he was leaving his seat and coming right up the aisle toward her!

"Go, Tiffany!" Mrs. Potter gave her daughter's shoulder a strong pat. Tiffany got up but stubbed her toe and stumbled into the aisle.

She crashed into the woman with the feather, who moved to her right. Tiffany

151

moved to her left. The woman moved left. Tiffany moved right.

"Will you get out of my way!" the woman with the feather barked, as Eddie leapt out into the aisle and grabbed for her. His flying tackle knocked her to the floor.

Amanda turned to the drummer behind her on the stage. "Hit the cymbals and let's sing it again!" she told him. The cymbals crashed, and the band launched into another chorus.

"Yo! Jack!" Eddie yelled from the floor, and, moving almost in a blur, Jack rushed to his side. The two of them helped the feather woman stand and then walked her up the aisle toward the exit, one on either side of her.

"Just kindly stop making such a scene," Jack told her quietly. To Eddie he said, "We'll ring the police. I'd already told them to stake out Mrs. Ditherfield's. Those girls are right toppers, eh?"

The woman with the feather was not happy.

"How dare you!" she was sputtering. "Both of you! And you, little girl!" She twisted around between Eddie and Jack and looked back angrily at Tiffany, who still stood gaping in the aisle. "I'll see to it that you never see the light of day again! You'll all be in jail so fast your heads will spin! How—How—" The feather woman began to stammer and then fell silent.

"But I didn't do anything!" said Tiffany. "I was just going to get a seat up front—"

"Tiffany!" Her mother was at her side and pushed her along the aisle to their seats.

Amanda watched all this from the stage, hoping that most of the audience was not aware of the commotion in the aisle.

Emily, still at the edge of the stage, was staring at Amanda. "What now?" she mouthed.

Amanda gestured for her to come up onto the stage.

Emily shook her head.

Amanda gestured again, frowning a little. It was an order. Amanda *was* a princess, after all.

Without a glance at anyone, Emily started for the stage. She reached the steps and rushed up them just as Amanda had done.

Emily was purple with embarrassment, but Amanda was her friend and they were in this together.

The Mashed Potatoes had almost finished their song when Emily appeared onstage beside Amanda. They could all hear the murmurs from the audience.

"Twins!"

"Oh, my—aren't they alike!"

"Will you look at their hair! Like copper!"

"Did you ever see such red hair!"

"Did you know there were twins in the family?"

Before the lead singer could announce the next song or thank the audience for their applause, Amanda held up her hand and walked to the center-stage microphone, pulling Emily along by the wrist.

"Eddie!" she mouthed, waving at the boy, who was still standing in the aisle, staring up at her.

"Me?" he mouthed, pointing to himself.

"Come up! Come up here!" Amanda called, gesturing. He moved. You don't argue with a princess, he knew.

As he was helped up to the stage, Amanda and Emily grabbed his hands and stood on either side of him.

"This is Eddie," Amanda said. "He's a great friend—"

Eddie's cheeks reddened.

"—but as it happens, he doesn't have a home. Eddie lives on the street."

Eddie bit his lip. He would have felt mortified, propped up on a stage with a bunch of rich people staring at him, hearing all about him—but he looked over at Amanda, then at Emily. He didn't feel bad. He felt lucky that some nice people really cared about him and wanted to help him. And his clothes were nice, weren't they? And, hey, right over there were the Mashed Potatoes!

But Amanda was still talking.

"We invited our friend Eddie so that you could see that the homeless people in the world are not nameless or faceless. There are real boys and girls out there, children like us, but not as lucky. They are innocent victims."

Tiffany shifted in her seat.

"That's a homeless boy!" her mother hissed at her.

"He's still cute!" Tiffany hissed back. "And besides, aren't we here because we *care*?"

"Anyway, our friend Eddie did a very courageous thing tonight," Amanda continued. "He's not the only innocent victim in this crowd." She looked toward the first few rows in the audience. "Mrs. Ditherfield, you are a kind, giving person, but someone wants to make a victim of you! Someone wants to rob you of your Queen Victoria necklace!"

There was a loud buzzing among the audience. Amanda quieted the noise with an upheld hand.

Uh-oh, Emily thought, here we go . . .

"And not only Mrs. Ditherfield, but others here tonight have lost some valuable treasures, too! We believe that a certain individual has been attending social gatherings in order to select wealthy victims to steal from. And we think we've stopped this individual tonight, with Eddie's help."

The audience began tentative applause.

Eddie and Amanda had given Emily more strength than she'd ever thought she had. She stepped closer to the microphone.

"Many of you have had things stolen from you . . . that is unfair. But what about taking from those who already have nothing?

We're here tonight to support those who need our help. We all have to think of others, not just ourselves. Whether it's helping to fix the roof of London's National Portrait Gallery or giving to the homeless, those who *have* really need to give lots."

Chapter Eleven

The thunder of applause made all three of them—Eddie, Emily, and Amanda—blush. They took one another's hands, and the Mashed Potatoes played one more chorus as Emily, Amanda, and Eddie smiled, waved, and left the stage.

The concert went on, of course. New York police officers held the woman with the feather in custody, while others who had already been dispatched to the Ditherfield mansion did indeed come upon two men, one with polished-looking hair, both dressed in black, climbing out onto the second-story balcony. They were carrying a soft black bag containing the Queen Victoria sapphire-and-diamond necklace, a diamond bracelet, and several platinum-and-diamond rings.

Backstage, while Pavarotti was singing "Vesti la giubba," two detectives talked with Amanda and Emily.

"So what tipped you?" one detective asked. "How'd you know who they were?"

"Who *were* they?" Amanda asked.

The detectives laughed. "No, seriously, Princess. How come you were the one who knew? And how come you didn't tell us before the concert?"

"Seriously," Amanda answered. "Who *were* they?"

The woman was Marjorie Mae Glintz, and Mr. Slick was her son, Buddy. They were the ones who managed to get onto the guest lists for the parties and sized up the art and jewelry. They were the leaders of a big jewelry and art theft ring but had no arrest records and were not suspected by the police. They

161

always brought along the others who would plan out and commit the actual theft. Then they'd meet later. The parties gave the two Glintzes the alibis they'd need later if they were questioned. Marjorie Mae wore the showy feather hats so that people would remember her and say they had seen her at the parties.

Amanda and Emily decided not to explain too well why the police had been sent to the Ditherfields'. If they revealed that they'd had no real evidence, they were afraid of what everyone would say.

"Just say we're protecting a source," Emily told Amanda. "They don't make you give up a source."

"What's a source?" Amanda wanted to know.

"I'm not sure, but they say it all the time on TV," Emily told her. "Anyway, you're a princess. Nobody's going to argue with a princess. Even if you *are* not quite eleven!"

Sitting on the piano at the after-concert party, the girls were the stars of the evening, even more than the famous performers. Everyone wanted to talk to them. Eddie came up and hugged them both, grinning from ear to ear.

A little later, Amanda found a moment to whisper to Emily, "It was kind, and very proper, of you to invite Tiffany Potter to the party."

"She did help stop the feather-head," Emily said.

"I'll never understand what made her stand up all of a sudden and get in the way," Amanda said.

Emily shrugged. "She was probably on her way to the bathroom! Anyway, it was lucky she stood up when she did. And then Eddie was right there. And Jack was terrific! He was so smart to have the Ditherfields' place staked out!" She shook her head in admiration. "By the way, I saw your parents speaking to you. Are they angry?"

"You know, I was watching Mummy's and Daddy's faces from the stage when I first got up there. . . ."

"Uh-oh," Emily said.

"But it's just fine. They realized that they'd raised so much money for the National Portrait Gallery's roof since we've been here, they can practically build a whole new museum! They're over the moon. This has been brilliant."

"Brilliant! It's been better than brilliant, Princess Amanda of Powers Court! My parents are ecstatic. This benefit puts them on the map forever. And not only that, but I got to spend time with you, and we saw New York City—"

"And we met Eddie, and I'm so pleased that he's going to stay with the Ditherfields. Wasn't that lovely of them to offer to take him in?"

"Mrs. Ditherfield said that with their kids

grown up, she's happy to have a young person around."

"And Eddie will watch over them, won't he?" Amanda said.

"Like a bulldog! He still can't believe it. And did you see something else that's hard to believe? Tiffany seems to have latched on to Eddie!"

Amanda laughed. "Emily, this has all been so wonderful," she said.

Emily laughed, too. "I feel as if I've been in a movie! We caught the bad guys, you got to see *and* sing with the Mashed Potatoes, and . . ."

"And?" Amanda asked.

"And," Emily said, "next time we're together, anything might happen!"

"I can't wait!" Amanda said.

About the Author

The Duchess of York has written two books with Benita Stoney on the life and travels of Queen Victoria: *Life at the Osborne House* and *Travels with Queen Victoria*. The Duchess's charity commitments include Children in Crisis and Chances for Children. The Duchess lives in London with her princess daughters.